Daredevil Doctors

Brothers, best friends...playboys!

After their brother Mick was left heartbroken at the altar and then suffered a life-changing injury in a tragic accident, brothers Eddie and James Grisham made a pact with him. From now on, they would seize life, take opportunities, chase adventure and—most importantly!—remain bachelors forever. Settling down and having their wings clipped is not an option...

Until one by one they meet their match in the most unlikely of places, and their resolve to remain single is tested... With their hearts opened to new possibilities, could an even more exciting future be on the cards for these daredevils?

Can Eddie's guarded colleague be the one to tame his heart in *Forbidden Nights with the Paramedic*?

And when a beautiful stranger arrives with news James is a father, he must face his fears and his future in *Rebel Doctor's Baby Surprise*.

Both available now!

Dear Reader,

Have you read one of my recent books called *Fling with the Doc Next Door*? With it being set in Scotland, along with my wonderful heroine Ella and her gruff but adorable Scottish hero, Logan, I think it might be one of my favorite stories so far. It was also where these two books began, because Ella was the big sister of triplets—Eddie, James and Mick.

After Mick was devastated at being jilted at the altar, these three brothers made a vow to be there for each other through thick and thin. They also vowed to avoid anything that could interfere with that bond and their determination to live their lives to the fullest—like a long-term commitment to any particular woman, for example.

It might not be intentional—or even welcome— but some of these vows are finally, dramatically, crumbling.

For all the gorgeous Grisham brothers. And for three amazing women who are about to change their lives forever.

Happy reading,

Alison xxx

Forbidden Nights
with the Paramedic

ALISON ROBERTS

HARLEQUIN
MEDICAL
ROMANCE

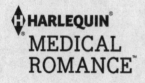

HARLEQUIN®
MEDICAL
ROMANCE™

Recycling programs
for this product may
not exist in your area.

ISBN-13: 978-1-335-59534-8

Forbidden Nights with the Paramedic

Copyright © 2024 by Alison Roberts

Harlequin Enterprises ULC
22 Adelaide St. West, 41st Floor
Toronto, Ontario M5H 4E3, Canada
www.Harlequin.com

Printed in U.S.A.

Alison Roberts has been lucky enough to live in the South of France for several years recently but is now back in her home country of New Zealand. She is also lucky enough to write for the Harlequin Medical Romance line. A primary school teacher in a former life, she later became a qualified paramedic. She loves to travel and dance, drink champagne, and spend time with her daughter and her friends. Alison Roberts is the author of over one hundred books!

Books by Alison Roberts

Harlequin Medical Romance

Morgan Family Medics

Secret Son to Change His Life
How to Rescue the Heart Doctor

Paramedics and Pups

The Italian, His Pup and Me

Miracle Baby, Miracle Family
A Paramedic to Change Her Life
One Weekend in Prague
The Doctor's Christmas Homecoming
Fling with the Doc Next Door
Healed by a Mistletoe Kiss

Visit the Author Profile page
at Harlequin.com for more titles.

PROLOGUE

THEY STOOD, shoulder to shoulder, in matching tuxedos at the front of the church.

Three men.

Three brothers.

Born thirty-two years ago, within minutes of each other, there'd never been any doubt that they would be together in such a significant moment in all their lives when the first of them, Michael, had decided to break their pact to remain bachelors for as long as possible.

Edward had come all the way from Australia, meeting James in London, where they'd both caught a train up to Aberdeen. It wasn't the town they'd grown up in but it was where their older sister, Ella, had chosen to make her life with the man she loved and that was close enough to a home base for three brothers who had never been ready to settle anywhere. Or with any*one*.

Until now.

Mick turned his head again, hoping to catch a glimpse of his bride, Juliana, preparing to walk down the aisle. His brothers instinctively turned as well, but the vestibule was still clearly empty. Instead, they shared a smile with Ella, who was sitting in the front pew, holding her husband Logan's hand.

Turning back to face the front, Eddie and James shared a glance that was brief but still spoke volumes.

They weren't completely comfortable being here. Sure, Mick was madly in love, but deciding to get married felt like a decision that had been rushed. A shotgun wedding?

What had happened to that pact they'd made after they'd lost both their parents when they were only teenagers—that life was too short and that they had to make the most of it—so, alongside an exciting career, they needed to cram in as many adventures and beautiful women as they could find? Just because this particular gorgeous girlfriend, whom Mick had met in Brazil on one of his recent deployments with *Médecins Sans Frontières,* was pregnant, it didn't mean they had to instantly commit to being together for the rest of their lives, did it?

Something didn't feel quite right.

And it seemed as if the brothers' disquiet was spreading throughout the small congregation in this church that was divided into a section with Michael's friends and family on one side and a few young Brazilian people on the other. Ella glanced at her watch and then whispered something to Logan. More than one of the guests on the bride's side of the church were turning their heads in the direction of the vestibule and one of them got up to walk outside, texting on his phone as he went.

The woman playing an organ began another rendition of Beethoven's 'Moonlight Sonata' and Mick's body language advertised an increasing tension.

'Brides love to be late,' Eddie reassured him quietly. 'It makes people even happier to see them walk down the aisle.'

Someone did appear but it wasn't the bride. It was the minister, who came through a side door close to where the brothers were standing. He smiled at Mick.

'Could you come with me for a moment, Michael?'

'What's wrong? Oh, my God…has something happened to Juliana?'

The minister's smile looked frozen now. 'Come to the vestry so we can talk in private.'

Eddie and James shared another glance. Privacy was not an option. Something was going on and they were not going to leave their brother without support. Ella and Logan were already on their feet, also ready to follow the minister and Mick.

The young Brazilian man who'd left the church a few minutes earlier was in the vestry.

'I am Juliana's brother, Lucas,' he told them. 'I'm sorry, but she cannot be here, after all.'

'Is she all right?' Mick had gone very pale.

'She is good,' her brother replied. 'Not unwell in any way.'

'So why isn't she here?'

Eddie and James moved closer on either side of Mick. Close enough for their shoulders to be touching.

It was the minister who broke a rather awkward silence by clearing his throat. 'It appears that there is someone else involved who arrived from Brazil this morning. The father of the baby Juliana is carrying.'

'*I'm* the father.' Mick sounded bewildered. 'She told me.'

Lucas shook his head. 'No. She was pregnant before she went to the medical centre where she met you. To José. He did not want to acknowledge the baby but now he has changed his mind. And Juliana is still in love with him. They are on their way to the airport to return to Brazil.'

Ella and Logan looked at each other. Then they looked at Mick.

'Stay here,' Ella said gently. 'Eddie and Jimmy

will stay with you until we've sorted everything and sent people home.'

An hour later the church was empty and the reception venue cancelled. Two hours after that, the brothers were in a hotel room and the first bottle of Scotch they'd ordered had just run dry.

'I'm calling room service,' Mick declared. 'We need another one of those.'

'Let's order dinner,' James suggested. 'Maybe some wine.'

'Champagne,' Mick muttered. His laughter held no amusement. 'Let's celebrate the fact I'm still single.'

'Hey, mate…' Eddie put his hand on Mick's shoulder. 'I know it hurts right now but you'll get past this. She wasn't the one for you.'

'Yeah…' James shook his head. 'Reckon you dodged a bullet there, bro. She was just using you to make her boyfriend jealous.'

'First and last time I'm getting married.' Mick shook his head. 'What was I thinking? We all know that life's too short and we need to live hard.' He raised his almost empty glass to his brothers. 'Take this as a warning and don't even go there.' He downed the last of his drink and grinned at them. 'Why settle down when there's a whole world to explore? And why buy a book when there's a whole library to enjoy?'

Eddie and James clinked glasses with him.

'Life *is* short.' Eddie nodded. 'Sometimes it's awesome and sometimes it sucks.' He draped his arms over each of his brother's shoulders. 'At least we've got each other. We can celebrate the awesome stuff and be there for each other for any of the bad stuff.'

The moment's silence following his words was verging on misty and Mick's voice was not much more than a whisper when he spoke.

'That's all we need,' he said.

CHAPTER ONE

Four years later...

'I'M NOT GOING BACK.' Edward Grisham shook his head slowly to underline his resolution. 'I can't.'

The man standing beside him in the hospital corridor was staring at him. Horrified.

'But you can't *not* go back,' he said. 'You've been here ever since the accident. Day and night. For *weeks*.'

'Exactly. That's why I can't go back.'

'So what am I supposed to tell your brother when he wakes up and you've just walked away?'

'I'm not leaving *Mick*, you idiot.' Eddie couldn't believe he'd been so misunderstood. 'I'm talking about not going back to *Australia*.'

'*Och*...' James Grisham tipped his head back as he blew out a breath that sounded relieved. 'Sorry...colour me sleep-deprived.' He threw a weary smile at Eddie. 'I've only had a couple of hours of shut-eye since a crazy busy night shift in Emergency last night. Let's go and get a coffee and you can fill me in properly.'

The route from the high dependency, acute section of this specialist spinal injury centre that was attached to Glasgow's Central Infirmary was all too familiar now but, on the plus side, they had discovered a small private courtyard not far from the cafeteria and, for a change, it was fine enough to get outside for a bit of fresh air. They ordered their coffee in takeaway paper cups and headed for a wooden bench that faced a small water feature in the courtyard garden.

'So…' James took another appreciative sip of the strongest coffee that had been on offer. 'You're going to leave your dream job with Air Rescue Australia?'

'Yep. Already have. I've got someone packing up my stuff to ship home as we speak.' He glanced at his watch. 'Or she will be when she wakes up and gets my message.'

'*She*…?' James raised an eyebrow. 'You leaving a girlfriend behind as well as your job?'

'Nah…that relationship was over a long time ago. Kylie and I are just friends now.'

'Keeping the pact, huh?'

Ah…that pact. The one that meant you never let a relationship get serious enough to interfere with what you wanted to do in your own life or worse, that would leave you in broken pieces when it crashed and burned—like Mick had been after he'd waited at the altar for a bride who was never going to arrive.

Not that any of the Grisham brothers had ever been disrespectful to women in any way. They'd always made it clear they weren't looking for anything serious. They made sure the chosen woman had as much fun as possible while they were enjoying their friendship with benefits and they almost always managed to leave before anyone got hurt and a continuing friendship—without the benefits—became unlikely.

The very idea of that pact, and the lifestyle that had fostered it, was becoming increasingly distasteful.

Eddie shrugged. 'I guess…'

'You don't sound too sure.'

Eddie rubbed his forehead with the pad of his middle finger. 'It's kind of changed everything, don't you think?'

'What? Mick's accident?'

'Yeah…'

'It's certainly changed everything for Mick.' James had to clear his throat as his voice roughened. 'What do you think the odds are that he'll be able to walk again?'

'You're the doctor, man. I'm only a paramedic. What do *you* think?'

The silence spoke volumes. Neither of them

wanted to discuss a worst-case scenario. They'd approached this journey as a family, one step at a time, ever since they'd first heard the awful news of Mick's serious accident when he was hang-gliding from the rugged slopes of Ben Nevis in the Highlands of Scotland. Mick had been flown by helicopter to this hospital and specialist spinal unit for his initial assessment and treatment and the family had gathered. James had been closest, currently working in an Edinburgh hospital, and he'd been waiting at the unit when Mick had arrived. It had taken Eddie thirty-nine hours to get here from Sydney, Australia, but he hadn't left since—thanks to the accommodation provided for close family members on the grounds of this centre.

That had been six weeks ago.

'He's due for some luck,' James said quietly. 'He's had just about every complication available so far, hasn't he?'

'I thought the worst was going to be seeing him in ICU on a ventilator when I came straight from the airport. Nobody warned me that I needed to buckle up for the rollercoaster that we've been on since then.'

'I know. Two rounds of surgery. Spinal shock, those cardiac complications of arrhythmias and, I don't know about you, but I found the levels of hypotension scarier than I wanted to admit. And then there was the paralytic ileus, pneumonia, unmanageable pain...'

Eddie's smile was wry. 'And I'd been so relieved to hear that the injury was incomplete. That it was at a thoracic level so he hadn't lost any sensation or function in his arms or hands. That there was a possibility he might walk again.'

'It might not feel like it but it's still early days.' James took a last mouthful of coffee. 'It could be weeks before he completely recovers from the spinal shock and who knows how much residual inflammation is there from both the injury and the surgery. At least he's stable enough to be able to be moved to a rehab centre in Aberdeen. At least Ella and Logan won't have that long drive so they can visit more often. Mick adores Ella.'

Eddie could hear a new level of concern in his voice now.

'I'm worried about how flat he's been in the last couple of weeks,' James added quietly. 'He's hardly eating. And I think all this sleeping might be a way of avoiding talking to us.'

'I've thought that too,' Eddie agreed. 'It wouldn't be surprising to have a clinical depression setting in after the initial fight to stay alive is done and dusted.'

'He's certainly showing some symptoms of depression.'

Eddie sucked in a breath. 'If anyone can help, it'll be Ella.'

Ella was the older sister of the triplet brothers. A second mother to them when they were growing up who'd married the love of her life a few years ago and was living and working in Aberdeenshire. She was the obvious anchor point for the brother who was going to need so much support from his family for the foreseeable future so it had been an easy choice to pick a centre in Aberdeen for the next stage of Mick's recovery and rehabilitation.

'And you're going to be a whole lot closer too?' James crumpled his cup. 'That's...' He gave Eddie a soft punch on his upper arm. 'That's awesome news, bro. Will you go and stay with Ella? Will you look for work around Aberdeen?'

'Don't need to.' Eddie took a deep breath. 'It seems that the universe was waiting for me to get back home. I've got a job lined up with the Aberdeen Air Ambulance—Triple A as they apparently like to call it—not to be confused with an abdominal aortic aneurysm.' He smiled at James. 'I can even take over the lease of an apartment from the medic I'm replacing.'

'Sounds perfect.'

'Yeah...' Eddie got to his feet. 'Hope so...'

James followed him back inside, his frown

advertising concern. 'You still don't sound too sure.'

Eddie shrugged. 'Like I said…everything's changed. It's like we've just been playing at being grown-ups until now. Going wherever we wanted in the world, doing the jobs that excited us the most.' He gave his brother a sideways glance that felt almost embarrassed. 'Making sure we stayed single so we could play the field like a bunch of irresponsible celebrities?' His sigh was heartfelt. 'Well…life got real the moment Mick fell out of the sky, didn't it?'

They walked back to Mick's room in silence but Eddie couldn't help thinking that he'd played a part in this whole catastrophe. He'd gone along with that pact that the three of them would live life to the fullest. That they'd avoid getting caught by a relationship or family responsibilities for as long as possible. That they'd grab every adventure they could in every part of their lives—their careers, their love lives and their hobbies.

Okay, Mick had taken it to a slightly higher level, but who could blame him after getting jilted like that and having to find a way through his heartbreak? It wasn't as if he or James had done anything to try and persuade him to tone it down. They'd listened to his stories about his work in dangerous places with *Médecins Sans*

Frontières, and his narrow escapes with his extreme sports like scuba diving and hang-gliding, and…and they'd been happy that he was loving life again.

But then it had all come crashing down. For Mick most of all, of course, but it was affecting every sibling of this close-knit family.

Everything had changed for them all and Eddie knew that their carefree, playboy, adventurous approach to life was most definitely one of the biggest changes.

Life *was* short, but that didn't mean you should give up caring about actually staying alive. Or the effect that pushing the limits might have on the people who loved you the most. Right now, it felt like their priorities had been off centre and the most important one—that family bond—hadn't been given the importance it deserved.

It felt like it might be time to grow up properly.

Jodie Sinclair had arrived at Aberdeen's Air Ambulance base, located at the far end of one of the runways of the city's main airport, even earlier than usual this morning and it wasn't just because that new coffee machine in the staffroom was so good.

Was it because she was feeling a wee bit nervous?

No… She shook her head at the ridiculous no-

tion as the discreet side door to the base build-
ings clicked open in response to the pin she
could only enter after her fingerprint was recognised by the biometric lock. Getting nervous
was on the list of negative emotional responses
that she'd learned long ago to dismiss before
they had any chance to affect her—profession-
ally or personally.

Jodie took a moment to look around the space
inside this vast hangar because this was what it
was all about, wasn't it? Right in front of her,
with its skids sitting on a large wooden platform,
was one of the sleek black H145 helicopters her
crew would be using today. The wheels on the
platform were on a length of railway line that
went beneath the roller door that ran the whole
width of the hangar and out to the helipad. With
just the press of buttons, the door could be raised
and the helicopter moved outside, ready to take
off at a moment's notice. That the destination
was still unknown and the emergency they were
being sent to was still a mystery was part of what
Jodie loved the most about this job.

She climbed a steel staircase that took her up
the wall of the hangar on the opposite side to
the winch training simulator that was the hull
of a helicopter fixed to a platform just beneath
the roof. It was part of the background that was
more than a second home for Jodie—it was the

setting for what was, without doubt, the most important part of her life.

Just arriving at work was enough for her to be focused. To feel that kind of anticipation that, for some people, might be close to excitement but, for Jodie, it was simply the space she needed to be in to do this job to the very best of her ability. She didn't need other people to tell her that she was at the top of her game. She didn't want them to, in fact, because there was always room to improve.

Unless something held her back.

Like a new crew partner who was a total stranger?

Someone who'd been working on the other side of the world. An Australian who might be trained as a paramedic and qualified to work on helicopters but could also be some kind of a cowboy who regarded protocols as merely guidelines. She'd seen those Crocodile Dundee movies with that laid-back hero with the lazy accent and the ridiculously large knife he carried around. If her new crew partner displayed the slightest hint of being a maverick like that, he was going to be in for some serious readjustment if he wanted to fit in to her crew.

The internal door from the hangar led directly into the staff area and, beyond, to the offices of the people who managed service operations, communications, maintenance and many other aspects of what it took to run a busy air rescue service. Jodie had been working here long enough to know everybody. Dion, the head of service operations who managed the day-to-day running of the base, was making a coffee for himself as Jodie went into the staffroom. Angus, one of their pilots, was sitting at a long table with a plate of toast and coffee in front of him. Alex, the crewman and co-pilot for their watch, was near the floor-to-ceiling windows of this space that was a great place to watch planes landing and taking off on the main runways of the airport.

'You ask him, Jodie,' Angus said. 'He won't tell me.'

'Ask him what, Gus?'

'Why he's still drinking that instant muck when he could be getting a really decent coffee from that new machine.'

'I know what I like,' Dion muttered. 'Why does everything have to keep changing?'

'I hear you.' Jodie grinned. 'But hey…it's only coffee. I've got to work with a new crewmate today and I haven't even met the guy.'

'You'll like him.' Dion opened the fridge to get a carton of milk. 'He flew through his orientation. I even rang the head of the base he worked at in Australia and they're gutted to be losing him. Told me we could count ourselves lucky he's decided to come back home to Scotland.'

'Back home? I thought he was an Aussie.' Jodie picked up a pod to slide into the coffee maker.

'He's as Scottish as the rest of us. Born and raised in Dundee, I believe. He's got a sister who's an obstetrician at Queen's, here in Aberdeen. Couple of brothers as well who are both doctors. High-flying medical family by the sound of it.'

'High-flying?' Angus spoke around a mouthful of toast. 'Pun intended?'

Jodie was watching the coffee trickle into her mug. 'We'll see,' she said. 'If I'd known you were going to appoint someone while I was away on holiday, I wouldn't have gone away.'

Dion's huff of laughter dismissed her claim. 'You're saying you would have given up your dream holiday of paragliding off Mont Blanc that you'd been planning for at least a year? I don't think so...'

Jodie grinned at him again. 'You do have a point.'

One of the lessons she'd learned long ago when the life she'd assumed she was embarking on had been ripped away from her, was that if you wanted life to mean anything at all you needed a goal to work towards. Preferably a big one. One that would take time and effort to reach. Even better, you'd have another one in place before the previous goal had been successfully dispatched. Not only bucket list holiday destinations for adventurous people but career goals as well.

Before leaving on her trip to the French Alps, Jodie had started putting plans in place to take her training to an even higher level that would take her to a Pre-Hospital Consultant Practitioner—a qualification that usually required the background of working as a doctor, not a paramedic. She was going to start by doing a PhD in paramedic science and already had topics under consideration with the appropriate academic committee. It might take a few years to get there but that made it possibly the best goal yet and...there wasn't anything else she wanted to do with her life, was there?

Alex turned away from the view and broke into her thoughts as the machine finished adding frothy milk to the espresso in her mug.

'So how was it?' he asked. 'That dream holiday of yours that would be most people's nightmare?'

'Unbelievable.' Jodie had been about to take her first sip of coffee but paused as the memory of that first jump filled her mind and sent a tingle throughout her body. She could feel, even more than hear, the exhilaration that coated her next words. 'You really haven't lived until you've tried jumping off a mountain like Mont Blanc. When you get the wind lifting your sail and then you turn and run and jump into nothingness, with nothing more than a nylon sail to keep you from falling thousands of feet onto the rocks. When you can sail over crevasses deep enough to hide a city as big as Aberdeen and close enough to glaciers to feel like you could reach out and touch them. It's the closest thing to flying that you could ever experience.' Jodie let her words fade into a sigh of happiness. 'It's the best feeling ever...'

She was turning as she spoke and she suddenly caught her breath, embarrassed by what must have sounded like an impassioned advertisement for the sport of paragliding to someone who didn't know her and probably wasn't the least bit interested in her recent holiday.

Someone like the man standing on the other side of the room, by the top of the staircase that came up from Reception? He was staring at Jodie as if she had been talking about something that wasn't simply over the top but possibly highly offensive.

A tall stranger who was dressed in the same uniform she was wearing herself. Heavy boots.

Black trousers with a tee shirt tucked into them. A black tee shirt with the logo of the Aberdeen Air Ambulance service beneath one shoulder and a small blue and white Scottish flag on one sleeve. Hair as dark as his clothing and facial features that were defined and eye-catching.

He was good-looking, there was no question about that, but that wasn't what was making this first impression of this man something completely out of the ordinary. There was a presence about him. A sense of calm, perhaps, that suggested he was totally in command of both himself and what was happening around him. For someone who preferred to remain in complete control herself, it was actually a little disturbing—as if a large rock was about to be thrown into the relatively calm pool of Jodie Sinclair's life.

So she stared back as if she could deflect anything that was potentially unwelcome. There might have been just a hint of defiance in her look that could well have contributed to the awkward silence that became apparent as the echoes of Jodie's enthusiastic response to the question of how her holiday had been evaporated. It was Dion who broke the silence.

'Eddie…come in.' He was smiling at the newcomer. 'Come and meet your crew partner and your pilot. Jodie, this is Edward Grisham. Eddie, this is Jodie, our chief paramedic.'

The stranger covered the gap between them with long, easy strides. It would have been rude to look away from him at this point but the steady gaze from a pair of eyes as dark as his hair seemed to be assessing her and, for some peculiar reason, Jodie felt her heart skip a beat—as if it mattered rather too much what he might be thinking of her? That was also disturbing...

'Good to meet you, Jodie,' he said, holding out his hand. 'I'm looking forward to working with you.'

His eyes advertised intelligence at this close range and that smile suggested he found it easy to make friends. Jodie, however, found it easy to ignore that kind of superficial charm and she was still a little rattled by her first impressions of her new partner, so it might have taken a beat too long for her to put her mug of coffee down on the table before taking his hand to shake it.

'Good to meet you too, Edward.' Her smile was one of genuine welcome but she wasn't about to offer the same assurance of looking forward to working with him. That would depend entirely on how good he was at his job—in real life, not according to a CV or hearsay or what he might think of his own abilities.

'Eddie, please...' He was still smiling at her.

'Or Ed. Only officers from Revenue and Customs tend to call me Edward these days.'

Jodie simply nodded. What she ended up calling her new colleague might also depend on how she felt about working with him but, in the meantime, it was quite nice to have a choice.

'Is there anything you'd like to go over before we start our shift? Any equipment you're not so familiar with, or protocols that are different to what you're used to?'

His gaze was level. 'I think I'm good, thanks. I might need to be reminded where things are for a day or two but I'm a quick learner.'

Jodie held his gaze and it felt like a challenge. 'Coffee's over there,' she said, tilting her head towards the bench. 'There's a pod machine or some very average instant. Milk's in the fridge. You've got plenty of time to grab a cup before our team briefing starts in the meeting room at six forty-five, but I'll be doing the drug check and restock for the shift in about five minutes. You might want to join me in the storeroom?'

She turned away to pick up her own coffee mug again and found Dion watching her, one eyebrow raised. Had she been rude, not offering to make coffee for their new team member?

Maybe. But guilt was another one of those emotions she had learned to control. She'd be more than happy to make a cup a coffee for Edward Grisham at some point.

He just had to earn that privilege first.

She wasn't tall. Five foot five at the most, given that the top of her head would barely reach Eddie's shoulder. And there was no getting away from noticing that she was seriously...*cute*.

Oh, man... Honed over the last couple of decades, Eddie had a skill that had become so automatic he was barely aware of his ability to absorb every detail about the appearance of a woman within the first few seconds of meeting her. He noted Jodie's height and the way her crew tee shirt hugged her curves. How the short style for her dark auburn hair suited her round face and that she had freckles she hadn't bothered to disguise scattered all over her nose and the top of her cheeks.

Her physical appearance was only the background impression Eddie was getting, however. There was something else about her that he could feel like a punch in his gut. Something almost compelling.

Did Jodie Sinclair have this effect on everybody?

Did that explain the slightly odd conversation he had had with the station manager, Dion, during his recent orientation days?

'You'll be working with Jodie Sinclair,' he'd told Eddie. *'Outstanding paramedic who's about your age.'* An eyebrow had been raised. *'A female partner's not likely to be a problem for you, is it?'*

Eddie had blinked in surprise. *'Why on earth would it be?'*

Dion had looked a little embarrassed. *'It's just a bit of a sensitive issue around here. We had a crew on another watch that, shall we say, imploded due to a relationship that was going on between crew members. A patient's care was put at risk while they were having some...ah... personal issues.'* He'd given Eddie a stern look. *'That's never allowed to happen again. Not on my watch.'*

Eddie had assured Dion that he had nothing to worry about and he'd meant every word he'd said. Besides, there were more important things to be aware of in this first meeting with Jodie than any physical attributes. Maybe it was something professional about his new partner that he was finding so compelling? Like the impression of intelligence and that gleam in Jodie's eyes that told him she liked being in charge. And that he was being assessed just as rapidly as he was assessing her.

Fair enough.

Eddie had found an article online last night

about this rescue base that contained profiles of the team members and Jodie's skills and achievements had been described in glowing terms. As an advanced practitioner in critical care, she had done extensive postgraduate training in pre-hospital medicine, completed a master's degree in paramedic science and gained high level qualifications in therapeutic procedures and drug administration. She might be a couple of years younger than Eddie but she was very definitely his senior as far as rank was concerned.

He had no trouble respecting that authority. He was quite prepared to earn any respect he might be given in return and he was more than happy to forgo a cup of coffee to be in the storeroom with her to go through the medication packs, which was just as well because he knew damn well that that had been an instruction rather than an invitation.

What Eddie was having a little difficulty with as he started this first day on his new job was what he'd overheard her saying as he'd arrived, when she'd been talking about hurling herself off one of Europe's most prominent mountains. Or, rather, it was the way she'd been talking about it, her tone dismissing any dangers inherent in the activity because of the pleasure it provided.

Just the way Mick used to talk about every new extreme sport he'd thrown himself into in the last few years. She must have seen the life-shattering consequences of bodies being badly broken or people losing their lives even when they weren't flirting with the dangers for pleasure. Eddie had to hope that it was just bravado that was making her sound so blasé about it. Or that he was overly sensitive on the subject right now because of Mick.

He had to work with this woman. In a profession that relied heavily on following safety procedures to the letter. Eddie was all too aware of how quickly the conditions in a mission could change. Given her seniority to him, his own life could depend on the decisions that Jodie would have the final say on and it wasn't the best start to have a warning light flashing in the back of his mind.

He was quite prepared to trust her. But trust had to be earned.

CHAPTER TWO

BY THE TIME he was halfway through his first shift with Aberdeen Air Ambulance's Blue Watch, Edward Grisham was confident that his new crew could well turn out to be up there with the best people he had ever worked with. Gus, the pilot, and their crewman, Alex, were both obviously highly experienced and competent in their roles and were disguising any wariness about the new boy at school with a friendliness that was very welcome. He could understand their curiosity about him and was quite happy to answer their questions about his time in Australia and his background when they stopped for a meal break.

'So you grew up in Dundee?'

'I did. With my older sister, Ella, and my two brothers.'

'Older or younger brothers?'

'Well, technically, they're both older than me but only by a few minutes. We're triplets.'

'No way...' Even Jodie had been startled by

that information and the curiosity in her eyes as she glanced up from her paperwork made Eddie notice their colour properly for the first time. Her eyes were brown but a much lighter shade than his own. A kind of milk chocolate sort of brown. The same warm colour of those freckles, in fact.

Nice…

'So you got cloned before you were even born.' Alex looked impressed.

'We're not identical. Ella's dad died when she was a baby and our mum got married again when Ella was about six years old. She and Dad wanted a baby of their own but nothing was happening so they tried IVF. Didn't work the first time with two eggs so they talked their doctor into chucking another one in on the next round for luck.'

'And they got three of you?' Gus was grinning. 'Your poor mother.'

'Ella was eight by then so she was like a second mum to us.' He made a face. 'I think it might have put her off ever having her own kids.'

'What was it like?' Jodie sounded still curious. 'I had friends at school who were twins and I always thought that was special. You're the first triplet I've ever met.'

Eddie rather liked the way she was looking at him as if *he* could possibly be something special himself. He wanted Jodie to like him, he realised. So he held her gaze for a heartbeat longer as he gave her the smile that he had every reason to believe made women melt at least a little.

'We were a pretty wild little pack by all accounts. Ella loves telling the story of how we nicked Mum's nail scissors and gave each other haircuts when we were about three years old. She says we thought the whole escapade was even more hilarious when she told us it looked like someone had run over our heads with a lawnmower.'

Jodie didn't return the smile. 'At least you didn't come back from Australia with a mullet.'

She went back to her paperwork, having dismissed his childhood reminiscence. It was definitely time Eddie stopped talking about himself and it was clearly far too soon to expect to hear any snippets of his senior paramedic partner's early years.

She wasn't being unfriendly despite not smiling back. And he hadn't found anything to account for that niggling disquiet about her during their work together so far today.

Jodie Sinclair was just as competent as Gus and Alex. She was focused, quick but efficient, and seemed to be following protocols to the letter so automatically that it was easy to work with her. Not that they'd faced any particularly challenging missions so far—two interhospital transfers, a man with an evolving myocardial infarct who needed urgent treatment that a rural clinic couldn't provide and a car accident that had ended up not needing the skills of the air rescue crew for the minor to moderate injuries involved.

Not that Eddie had any concerns about how this crew would respond to a serious event. Not at all. He was looking forward to being part of such a call-out, in fact. It was just that...

...that something was still bothering him. Nothing he could put his finger on, exactly, but it was there at the back of his mind. An unknown. Perhaps it was because of a natural wariness on both sides as to how this crew would gel when they were tested with more than simply routine work. Or maybe it was a leftover antipathy from early this morning to the way he'd heard her talking about hurling herself off mountains. She might be winning some trust on a professional level but, personally—despite that curiosity about his own upbringing as a triplet, she was still a stranger.

Maybe his disquiet was due to the fact that what was bothering him felt like a warning of some kind.

One that went up a notch, for some reason, when the call he'd been hoping for came through just after their lunch break.

'It's near Fort William,' Dion told them, coming into the staffroom as their pagers were sounding. 'Closer to Glasgow than us, but currently we're the only chopper available. A mountain rescue team has been activated but it's going to take them some time to get to the scene. Sounds like the access is going to be a wee bit gnarly.'

The crew were already moving—heading for the staircase that led down to the hangar, their boots clattering on the steel treads.

'Mountain biker,' Alex relayed, managing to read a screen as he kept moving. 'Hit a log on a downhill run and went headfirst over the handlebars.'

'Head, neck and chest injuries.' Jodie was first into the cabin of the helicopter and clicking her harness into place as Eddie climbed in after her.

'Have we got a GCS?' he asked.

'Apparently fifteen,' Jodie responded. 'Conscious and alert. The other rider with her is making sure she's not moving but she's in a lot of pain.' She fastened the strap of her helmet. 'Gus? What's our ETA?'

'Twenty minutes flight time or thereabouts.' Their pilot's voice was loud and clear in the helmet's inbuilt headphones. 'But we can't know your ETA to the patient until we have a look at what the access is like. I've been in the area before and winching you in might not be an option, given the tree cover and the wind gusts we're getting today.'

Twenty minutes was more than enough time to remind himself of everything important Eddie had learned or dealt with when it came to potential head, chest and neck injuries. He knew they would have to check carefully for any major trauma and that anything compromising the airway or circulation took precedence over a potential spinal injury. He knew the whole raft of interventions and drugs that could be used to stabilise the patient enough to move them to the nearest major trauma unit in a tertiary hospital. He knew how to ensure the patient was appropriately immobilised, positioned and protected from any secondary injuries for that transport.

But this felt completely different to any other call he'd had to an accident like this.

Because of Mick.

Because he now had personal experience of just how life-changing an accident like this could be. Eddie had always been aware of the weight of responsibility that came with the job he did. Aware of the power he had to change the course of the rest of someone's life. Or even save that life. But this was the first possible spinal injury he would be assessing since Mick's accident and that awareness was so acute, his adrenaline levels were high enough to be making his heart speed up and his mouth feel dry.

As if he was nervous?

It didn't help that the glance Jodie gave him suggested that she'd picked up on the tension he was feeling. Eddie knew she would be assessing every action of his along with her assessment of the scene and their patient. Nobody wanted a nervous crew partner. It also didn't help that, as they circled the GPS co-ordinates they'd been given, it became apparent that Gus had been correct. There was no obvious place to land close to the scene and the tree cover on the steep hill was so dense it took some time to even catch a glimpse of the high vis vests the mountain bikers were wearing. A winch operation was well out of any safety boundaries.

'There's a clearing beside that hut on the summit,' Gus pointed out. 'I can land us there but you're going to have to carry your gear down the track from there.'

'The mountain rescue team are already on the track heading uphill,' Alex added. 'They're carrying a basket stretcher which will make it easier to carry her back up.'

The on-board portable stretcher was one less thing the crew needed to carry downhill, but they were approaching a patient who'd had a significant mechanism of injury and whose condition could well have deteriorated since their last update. They had to carry a life pack and oxygen, equipment to deal with any serious airway or breathing issues from an intubation kit to a suction device and a portable ventilation unit, as well as many other items, including IV gear, drugs, tourniquets, splints and dressings. Gus would be staying with the helicopter but there were packs for each of the others to carry and it didn't escape Eddie's notice that Jodie reached to pick up the largest one.

'I can take that,' he said.

Her quick glance told him the offer was neither needed nor welcome. She slipped her arms through the straps and had clipped the belt buckle into place by the time Eddie and Alex had gathered the rest of the gear and then led the way towards the track opening from the clearing, with a quick look over her shoulder to make sure the men were keeping up with her.

Eddie lengthened his stride.

The real test had just begun, hadn't it?

Jodie was watching her new colleague carefully but not overtly, with a sideways glance here and a look over her shoulder there when he might not expect it. Something had been bothering her ever since she'd noticed how tense he was on their flight to this scene, thanks to that bunched muscle in his jaw that told her he was gritting his teeth and the way his hand clenched into a fist when he wasn't using his fingers to scroll through the information coming in on their tablets. She hadn't considered him to be showing any nerves so far today, so what was so different about this job? Given his track record, he had to be experienced enough in being dispatched to a trauma case of unknown severity for it not to be a problem. Was his current level of tension because this was the first case that might demonstrate to his new colleagues just how good he really was at his job?

If so, and he did have anything to worry about, Jodie wanted to know exactly what it was.

After a sometimes slippery and unpleasantly steep descent on a few parts of this mountain biking trail, they had arrived at the scene of the accident and Jodie deliberately held back to let Eddie approach their patient first.

The young woman was lying on her back amongst rocks on the side of the trail, covered with a coat and with a woollen jumper folded and tucked under her head. A young man wearing only a tee shirt was holding the helmet she was still wearing, to keep her head still. Eddie nodded at him but crouched low so that the woman could see his face.

'Hey…' The tone of his voice was as reassuring as a smile. 'You're Caitlin, yes?'

'Y-yes…'

'Sorry we took so long, sweetheart.'

Ohh… Beneath that Crocodile Dundee casualness, as if they were just a bit late for a coffee date or something, Jodie could actually *feel* his sincerity. If he was acting, he'd nailed it well enough to win an Oscar. If she was in Caitlin's position hearing those words and seeing his face that close to her own, she would feel as if she was the only person who mattered in the world in this moment.

And what better way to feel when you were in pain and frightened and had no idea what was about to happen to you? Even if that was the only contribution Eddie was about to make to the management of this patient, making her feel that she was about to taken care of by someone who cared this much was priceless.

'I'm Eddie,' he was saying now. 'And I've got Jodie and Alex with me. We're going to look after you, okay?'

'O-okay…' Caitlin was shivering, despite the extra coat over her shoulders. And then she started crying. 'It hurts…'

'What's hurting the most for you?'

But Caitlin was dragging in a breath following a sob and couldn't get any words out. Jodie could see that Eddie was doing a rapid assessment. He shone his pen torch across both eyes to check pupil size and reaction and moved the jacket covering Caitlin, gently unzipping the one she was wearing underneath, so he could watch the way her chest was moving as she breathed. He put his fingers on her wrist, checking for a pulse, and Jodie knew he was taking in her colour and heart rate, and an idea of how low her blood pressure might be at the same time as scanning the surrounding rocks for any evidence of blood loss.

Jodie was doing the same thing as she was opening their packs and getting gear out. She nodded approvingly at Alex, who had also taken in the first impressions and was ripping open the package for a foil blanket. They *had* taken a while to get here and hypothermia was a risk factor. He had the vacuum mattress kit on the ground beside him as well, which was their best bit of equipment for moving a patient with suspected spinal injuries.

'It's her neck.' It was Caitlin's companion who answered for her when she just groaned again. 'And I think she's hurt her ribs because she said it hurt her to breathe and…and she's going to be okay, isn't she?' His face was ashen. 'She was going so fast when she hit that log and she landed on her head and just flipped over like a pancake and landed on these rocks. I've been too scared to let her move and…and it's taken so long for you guys to get here.'

'I know… I'm sorry. What's your name, mate?'

'Ian.'

'Good job keeping her warm and still, Ian. And getting help on the way. Was Caitlin knocked out by the fall?'

'She was a bit out of it, but not really unconscious. Just groaning and stuff.'

'You're a friend of Caitlin's?'

'We're getting married next year.'

'Hey…' Eddie was smiling again. 'Congratulations. Caitlin? Can you hear me?'

'Mmm…' The sound was a stifled groan.

'Can you squeeze my hand?'

Eddie's gaze flicked up to meet Jodie's but she could see there was no movement at all in Caitlin's hand as it lay completely limp inside his.

But Eddie gave hers a squeeze. 'That's great,' he said. 'I'm going to get your helmet off now, very carefully, and we're going to put a collar around your neck. I'm going to take care of your head so nothing moves that shouldn't, but we do need to shift you a wee bit to get you off these rocks and onto something more comfortable while we find out properly what's going on.'

'*No*…' Caitlin had tears rolling down her cheeks. 'Please don't move me… It hurts…'

'We're going to take care of that pain for you right now, sweetheart. Are you allergic to anything that you know of?'

'No…'

'Are you on any medications at the moment or have any medical conditions we should know about?'

'No…'

Eddie got to his feet again. 'Ian, I'm going to take your spot at Caitlin's head there so I can look after her neck, but we're going to need your help when we lift her off these rocks, okay?'

'Okay.'

'You go down by her feet so you can be ready to help lift in a minute or two. Jodie, can we get some pain relief on board for Caitlin, please? And, Alex, could you come and hold her head steady while I get this helmet off? Throw me a collar too, thanks.'

Jodie slipped a cannula into a vein on Caitlin's arm. If her blood pressure was as low as was indicated by how hard it was to feel her radial pulse, their patient was going to need more than IV pain relief. She would need fluids and drugs to maintain enough blood pressure to keep her spinal cord perfused.

It was automatic to warn about the sharp scratch of the needle but her heart sank when it was obvious how little sensation Caitlin had in her upper limbs. It meant that her spinal injury was at a high level and, while it was impossible to know what the prognosis was when these signs could be due to something temporary like spinal shock, it was an ominous sign. It also meant they needed to keep a sharp eye on her breathing and it was an indication that intubation might well be necessary to look after her airway and keep her still enough during transport to avoid any additional damage when they couldn't know how unstable a spinal fracture might be.

Eddie had to be thinking about the same things, judging by how serious his face was as he directed everybody's hand positions and issued instructions for how and when they moved, while he took responsibility for keeping her cervical spine in line with the rest of her spinal column as they did a log roll to get Caitlin onto the vacuum mattress that Alex had pumped air out of to make it a stiff board.

'Up on the count of three,' Eddie ordered. 'One, two...*three*...' He had his hands splayed on either side of Caitlin's head to make sure her neck bones stayed in line with the rest of her spine as she was turned.

Caitlin cried out in pain but, in her position controlling the shoulders, it was possible for Jodie to steady her body against her legs as she ran her fingers down her spine to check for any obvious deformities or painful areas. There was no bleeding that she could see. With Ian's assistance they tucked the stiff mattress behind Caitlin and then it was time to turn her back again.

'Down on the count of three.' Eddie's face was so focused it looked almost grim now. 'One, two...*three.*'

They could slide the mattress onto flat ground now, away from solid objects like smaller rocks that could cause problems. They let air back into the mattress so it could conform to her body shape and then took enough out for it to shrink and provide immobilisation support while they did a rapid but thorough primary survey, assessing breath sounds and chest movement more accurately and attaching monitoring equipment to get baseline measurements of blood pressure, oxygen saturation and heart rhythm.

With that done, and the timely arrival of the mountain rescue team with their carrying power and expertise in navigating difficult terrain for an extrication, they were ready to take the remaining air out of the mattress and secure the straps which would provide the safest immobilisation and meant that Caitlin could be easily lifted into the basket stretcher the mountain rescue team was carrying. The high sides of the plastic basket and all the handholds were designed to help carry someone up steep terrain like this and having Caitlin cocooned in the vacuum mattress would make the switch to the helicopter's stretcher seamless.

Eddie bent the top of the air mattress closer to Caitlin's head as it shrank to provide the same kind of support that sandbags or blocks could offer, but Jodie suddenly signalled Alex to stop pumping.

'Wait…' She glanced at the monitor where an alarm was beeping and then at Caitlin's chest. Her breathing rate had increased but it was still shallow and her oxygen saturation was falling, despite having oxygen running into the mask she was wearing.

'I don't want her head secured yet,' Jodie said quietly. 'I'm not happy with her respiratory effort.'

'Caitlin?' Eddie leaned down, close to her ear. 'Can you open your eyes for me?'

There was no more than a flicker of her eyelashes. Caitlin had been drowsy since they'd administered powerful drugs to control her pain but this was a deeper level of unresponsiveness.

'Blood pressure's down to eighty-five over fifty.'

'SpO2's under ninety.'

'She's tachycardic.'

'Respirations well over thirty.'

Eddie caught Jodie's gaze. 'You want to intubate?'

She gave a single nod, which he mirrored. It was obvious to both of them that getting control of her airway before they packed up their gear and started what could be a slow and difficult climb up the hill was a no-brainer. She needed another fluid bolus and medication to try and bring her blood pressure up as well. Alex was already getting the airway pack open and the laryngoscope was visible, along with its blades and the plastic tubes that would secure an airway. The small portable ventilator unit they had carried down with them was waiting to one side as well.

The mountain rescue team were looking after Ian. He had his warm coat back on and someone had provided a hot drink. They were also supporting him as it became obvious that his fiancée's condition was more serious than he might have realised.

Eddie was already at their patient's head, in the perfect position to do the intubation.

'I'll stabilise her neck from underneath,' Jodie said. 'You happy to do the intubation?' It wasn't really a question. She was already in position to assist rather than take the lead in this procedure. She was leaning in, ready to steady her elbows on Caitlin's chest and put her hands around her jaw bones to keep her head steady when Eddie's response made her stop in her tracks.

'No,' he said.

Jodie blinked. 'What?'

She was actually confused for a split second. Had her new *junior* crew partner just refused to do what she'd requested? In a tone that had been flat enough to suggest he had no intention of changing his mind or even discussing it? He had been looking down at Caitlin's face between his hands as he spoke and he still hadn't raised his glance so he couldn't see Jodie's incredulous expression.

'I'm not moving until we've got her secured,' he said. 'You can work around me to remove the collar and then intubate, yes?'

Jodie could feel Alex's startled glance but didn't look in their crewman's direction. This wasn't the time to comment on not only Eddie's refusal to follow her directions but telling her what to do. That would most certainly come later, but right now there were far more important things to focus on and yes…she could work around and through the position of his arms.

It did mean, however, that she had to crouch close enough beside Eddie for her hip to be pressing against his leg and her arms to be repeatedly touching his and she wasn't that comfortable being close to someone that she clearly couldn't trust to work with her the way she was entitled to expect, but this was also not the time to even think about that. They had work to do and they needed to do it swiftly.

The first task was to carefully undo the straps holding the cervical collar closed because it would make it impossible to open the mouth far enough for the procedure. With her arm leaning on his to steady herself, Jodie could feel how rigidly Eddie was holding Caitlin's head still as she worked. Alex was busy drawing up the drugs needed to anaesthetise and paralyse their patient.

The intensity of Eddie's focus as he provided just enough tilt, and not a millimetre more, to let her insert the laryngoscope blade and then stylet and the plastic tube was, quite literally, palpable. It might have influenced the way Jodie also concentrated, completing the procedure smoothly and swiftly and then securing the tube, attaching oxygen and setting up the ventilator. It was only after the air mattress was flattened onto either side of Caitlin's head that he finally moved his hands. And it was only then that he looked up to make eye contact with Jodie.

And he looked…angry?

Jodie stared back for a heartbeat. What was going on here? She was the one who should be angry because he'd flatly refused to comply with her request as the senior paramedic on scene. It was insupportable and she was going to have a chat with Dion when she got back to base because she wasn't at all sure she wanted to work with this newcomer.

One member of the volunteer mountain rescue team was going to take Ian—and the two bicycles—down the track and get him back to his own vehicle so that he had transport to get to the hospital.

'Where are you going to take Caitlin?' he asked.

'The closest major trauma centre will be Glasgow, and that will be the very best place she can go because there's a specialist spinal unit attached to the hospital. We'll be able to let you know before you get back to your car.'

The only communication made on the trip back up the track between everybody involved was information being shared, from monitoring Caitlin's condition, radio communication to arrange their destination and give Gus a heads-up that they would be taking off soon and directions from the mountain rescue team as they passed the stretcher from hand to hand to get it over narrow gaps between large boulders and muddy slopes that could have been dangerously slippery.

Jodie was the one who was angry now but, like any negative emotion, she had it completely under control, well in the background, and it was easy to keep it completely private by avoiding direct eye contact with Eddie and focusing absolutely on their patient. By the time they landed on Glasgow's Central Infirmary's roof helipad, however, the issue simmering at the back of her mind had led to a decision.

Edward Grisham might not have come back from Australia with a mullet hairstyle but he'd picked up an attitude that was unacceptably arrogant.

Or maybe he'd always been like that?

Whatever. He was a cowboy. A maverick. Someone who was going to do what *he* wanted to do, no matter what anyone else had decided was the best course of action. And maybe it hadn't done any harm in this instance but, as far as Jodie was concerned, it meant their partnership was not going to work and she had every intention of marching into Dion's office the moment they got back on base and asking him to arrange to swap Eddie onto a different watch.

It was Jodie who gave a detailed handover to the emergency department consultant and the specialist orthopaedic surgeon from the spinal unit who was amongst the team waiting for them. They were complimented on their management of Caitlin so far and as the emergency department staff handed back their vacuum mattress and were busy setting up their own monitors, Jodie turned away, reaching to start pushing their stretcher from the trauma resuscitation area, satisfied that they had done their best for this patient.

And then she froze.

The surgeon was stepping towards Eddie. Shaking his hand.

'I thought I'd seen the last of you, Ed,' he said.

'Me too, Andrew.'

Jodie could feel her eyes widening. Her new colleague was on first name terms with a Glaswegian specialist orthopaedic surgeon? More than that, there was a feeling that they shared something that was significant to both of them. What was going on?

'First day on my new job in Aberdeen,' Eddie added with a wry smile. 'Guess I can't keep away from this place.'

The surgeon was returning the smile but his frown advertised concern. 'How's Mick?'

The shadow crossing Eddie's face was noticeable. 'Ah…you know. Still settling in. It's…not easy…'

'I know. Keep in touch, won't you? Let me know if I can help in any way.'

'Will do, thanks.'

Eddie didn't look at Jodie as they took the stretcher to the nearest lift to get back to the roof, where Gus and Alex were waiting to take them back to base. She was at the back of the stretcher and she found herself staring at Eddie's back as he pressed the button to take them up. The silence in the lift as the doors closed felt heavy and Jodie took a deep breath. She knew perfectly well that she might be crossing a boundary between professional and personal but this felt important.

'Who's Mick?' she asked.

Eddie didn't turn around. 'My brother.'

Another silence fell that lasted as the lift slowed to stop at another floor. When the waiting nurses saw that it was already filled with a stretcher and two people, they stood back and the doors slid shut again.

'Mick's just spent a couple of months in the spinal unit here,' Eddie said quietly. 'He had a hang-gliding accident up in the Highlands.'

It took only a second for several things to fall into place.

The way Eddie had been looking at her when he'd arrived this morning, when she'd been raving about how life-affirming it was to be jumping off mountains. The tension he'd been showing on that flight to their last patient. That fierce determination that nothing was going to interfere with his protection of her neck so that her potential injury was not exacerbated in any way.

In the same instant, Jodie could see herself the way Eddie must have been seeing her. As someone with little respect for the sanctity of life. Possibly with less respect than she actually felt for protecting the life of a patient in her care. She could even hear an echo of the sharp tone in her voice when she'd responded to his refusal to move his hands from Caitlin's head.

Thinking that they weren't actually suited to be working together was probably not one-sided and…and she couldn't really blame Eddie if he might be wondering if he'd made a mistake coming to work at Triple A.

Worse, she didn't like the glimpse she was getting of herself through his eyes.

Eddie cleared his throat. 'His injury's not as high as Caitlin's but it's still going to be a long road back to recovery.' The lift was slowing again as it reached their destination. 'That's why I've moved back from Australia. And why I've taken the job in Aberdeen. Mick's just been transferred to a rehabilitation centre there.'

It was in that instant that Jodie realised he hadn't been acting in that sincerity he'd displayed with Caitlin. If the bond that had to be there with his brother was enough for Eddie to have overturned his whole life in order to be close enough to support him for as long as he was needed, then he was more than capable of caring as much as he'd appeared to for a patient.

There was a single word that she could hear in the back of her head right now.

Sweetheart...

Nobody had ever called Jodie 'sweetheart'. Not even Joel. But they'd practically grown up together, dating since high school, and their endearments were more likely to be cheeky than cheesy. He'd called her 'short stuff'. Or 'spot', because of her freckles. But it hadn't mattered because their love was rock solid. They were going to be together for life.

Until they weren't...

The lift shuddered to a halt and there was that tiny bit of time before the doors opened that might be the last private moment Jodie had with Eddie before they were sucked back into the noise and busyness of the rest of their shift. She needed to say something, but Jodie's thoughts were very uncharacteristically tangled.

Those memories of Joel certainly hadn't helped, but she'd already been messed up with a level of emotion she would never normally allow to happen.

Ever.

She wasn't about to let it happen for a moment longer either. Because, if it did, it would take her even further back, to a space she had fought so hard to get away from, a very long time ago. The time when her life had been intact.

As perfect as she'd ever hoped it would be.

'I'm sorry,' was all she said as the door slid open onto the roof.

It was more of a mutter, really. Maybe because Jodie wasn't exactly sure what it was she was apologising for.

The devastating accident that one of his brothers had experienced?

For coming across as being…what…flippant, perhaps?

For not being able to express, or even feel, the level of emotion that Eddie was obviously capable of?

For having decided that she was going to make a request to not have to work with him any longer?

No…

The apology was for all of those things, but it was also because she had misjudged him. And, if she was really honest with herself, was it because she was sorry she wasn't more like him herself? Someone who had attributes on a personal rather than a professional level that were admirable. Attractive, even…?

It would be all too easy to resent someone who'd held up a mirror to show her something that she didn't like about herself, but Jodie wasn't going to allow herself to do that. She could work with this man and not let anything personal affect their professional relationship.

When they settled in to working together they could, in fact, make a great team with the way they could complement each other's skills, which was a much more positive way to view what had happened. It wasn't as if his refusal to follow her direction on their last case had compromised the care of their patient in any way. It could even be argued that she was partly to blame herself when she had, after all, phrased her request by asking if he was happy to do the procedure. He'd had good reason to say he wasn't, so she should just let it go.

As long as it didn't happen again.

Jodie ducked her head as they pushed the stretcher towards where Alex was waiting to help them stow their gear beneath the rotors on the helicopter that were already gaining speed.

'We've got another call to make on the way home,' Alex told them. 'A paediatric transfer from a medical centre in Laurencekirk. Respiratory distress probably due to bronchiolitis, but there are concerns about whether the kid's stable enough to send by road.'

Jodie felt something very like relief as she heard the stretcher wheels lock into position and she could sit down and strap herself in for the flight. It was one of the best things about this job—there was always something just around the corner that could completely distract you from dwelling on anything remotely personal.

CHAPTER THREE

HE WASN'T GOING to let it bother him.

That less than sympathetic apology from Jodie Sinclair when he'd told her about Mick's accident. Or the carefully professional distance she'd been keeping from him ever since.

What had he expected? Some real interest in his personal life? Some genuine concern for the difficulties his brother—and therefore his whole family—were facing? Perhaps he'd hoped that telling her might break the ice in getting to know each other better.

'It's not that she's not friendly,' he told his brothers when he visited Mick after his shift had ended. 'I'm just not sure she likes me much.'

It was a new experience for Edward Grisham. People tended to like him instantly. Especially women...

Was it that Jodie didn't like anyone much? That she was one of those rare women who were lone wolves?

He'd certainly got that impression with the

look she'd given him when he'd refused to let go of Caitlin's head in order to perform the intubation. He would have been happy to discuss it with her as a debrief when the mission had been completed, but he'd ended up working with Alex to clean and restock the gear in the helicopter cabin while Jodie disappeared into the secure storeroom to check and replenish the drug and airway kits.

He'd found her sitting at the table in the staffroom as their shift ended, completing the patient treatment report, but when he'd started speaking she'd held up a hand in an unmistakable gesture to stop him saying anything.

'Just give me another few minutes? I don't want to get any of these drug dosages or times incorrect.'

'No worries,' Eddie had said. 'It can wait. I need to head off, anyway. My brother James has come up from Edinburgh to visit Mick and I said I'd try and get to the rehabilitation centre to catch up with them both.'

Jodie had clearly stopped focusing on inputting her data, her fingers poised above her tablet keyboard. 'Of course. Go.' Her glance slid across his. 'See you tomorrow.'

Remembering the smile she had given him at that point was enough to make Eddie wonder now if he was overreacting. It had, after all, been his first day working with Jodie and perhaps he'd misinterpreted both that look and the lack of sincerity in that apology?

Judging by the amused sound from his brother James, he wasn't the only one who thought his impression might have been incorrect.

'Maybe she fancies you,' he offered. 'You know, like the girls at primary school that could be mean because they didn't want you to know they liked you that much in case you didn't like them back?'

'I *don't* like her back. Not like that, anyway. When I said I wanted to get to know her better, I wasn't talking about jumping into bed with her.'

James lifted an eyebrow. 'Because she's part of your crew? I get it. If she wanted more than something casual, it could get a bit awkward in a confined space like a helicopter cabin. At least I've got a whole emergency department to use if I want to create some distance.'

Had James not been listening the other day when Eddie had said how he felt as if everything had changed since Mick's accident? That what was important in life suddenly seemed to be something a lot deeper than skating through life in a completely self-centred way, working hard, focusing entirely on having an exciting career during work time and playing just as hard out of work hours, with as many gorgeous women as possible?

'You must have noticed how cute she is,' James added. 'Stunning, even. I was showing Mick that online article about her when I got here this afternoon. The one with the photograph of her standing beside the chopper with her helmet under her arm? Is she single?'

'I've got no idea. And I'm not about to ask.' Eddie shook his head slowly. 'And it's not just that there are some strict rules in place for not messing around with your crewmates. Don't you ever think that it's a bit…shallow—wondering if every beautiful woman you meet might be up for a bit of fun? That you might be hurting people even if they don't make it obvious? Or wasting time when you could be making a real connection with someone?'

James blinked. 'Not if they know you're not interested in anything more than a bit of fun. There's plenty of girls out there who are more than happy to play—as you well know.'

Eddie did know. And he didn't like that he knew.

'What's the point of making a "real" connection, anyway?' Mick's tone was bitter. 'That just means that *you're* the one that's going to end up getting hurt.'

It was always there, wasn't it? The memory

of that awful time at the wedding, when it became obvious that Mick's bride wasn't going to be making an appearance. Mick's devastation had been contagious and the bond between the three brothers had never felt so strong.

It felt like that again now. Eddie could sense how desperate James was to change the subject he'd been responsible for introducing.

'It wasn't just the photo,' he said. 'Sounds like your Jodie is a smart cookie. She seems to be set on becoming the highest qualified paramedic in Scotland. We were both impressed, weren't we, Mick?'

'Aye...'

But Mick didn't sound particularly impressed. Or interested. He was lying flat on his bed in his private room, with the wide doors that led out to a wheelchair accessible garden, staring at the ceiling—as he had been ever since Eddie had arrived. Mick's wheelchair was parked in the corner of the room, near the door to the en-suite bathroom.

'I'm sorry you're having to work with someone you don't like much,' Mick muttered. 'Or who doesn't like you.' He closed his eyes. 'You didn't have to leave the job you *did* like so much, you know. I never asked you to move back to hang around for me.'

'I know.' Eddie tried to sound offhand, but

he was kicking himself mentally for giving Mick the idea that he might be less than happy with his major life decision. 'I did it because I wanted to. It was time I came home again—I hadn't realised how much I missed Scotland. All this lovely rain...' He found a smile. 'I kind of missed you guys too, believe it or not.'

'Not.' But James was also smiling as he glanced at his watch. 'I'll have to hit the road before too long, if I'm going to get back in time to start my night shift. How 'bout we get you out of that bed and you give us a guided tour of this place, Mick? From what I saw on the way in, it looks pretty flash.'

'Great idea,' Eddie agreed, relieved that his new job—and his new partner—were no longer the focus of their conversation. 'I'd like to see the gymnasium and the pool and the games room. Is there a pool table in there?'

Mick shrugged, his eyes still closed. 'Wouldn't know. Haven't been able to sit in the chair long enough to go anywhere. They're still juggling my pain meds.'

'Have you got your timetable for all the therapy sessions?' Eddie asked. 'They told us they'd be giving you a thorough assessment after you'd had time to settle in and then the whole team would be meeting to draw up a plan for your individualised programme.'

Mick opened his eyes, which only made his expression bleaker. 'Apparently you lose a lot of muscle strength by lying around for too long. Who knew? My arms are like strings of spaghetti. I can't even turn the wheels of that chair.'

'You'll get there.'

'Get where, exactly? It's not like I can go back to a clinic in Ethiopia or be on standby for a natural disaster somewhere, is it?'

The silence between the brothers acknowledged how much had changed and Eddie's tone was gentle.

'Hang in there, mate. And don't even think about giving up hope yet. None of us know how much function you're going to get back. And, knowing what you're like, you're going to smash this challenge like everything else you've ever done in your life.'

'I'll get back up on my next proper day off,' James told Mick. 'But I'll give you a video call before then.' He picked up his leather jacket and motorcycle helmet. 'I'm keeping an eye out for a locum position up here too. Logan tells me the Emergency Department at Queen's is a good place to work. Hey... I could move into your apartment with you, Eddie. That'd be fun.'

Eddie shook his head. 'It's only got one bedroom,' he said. 'We might have shared a womb once, mate, but I'm not sharing my bed with you.'

Mick didn't join in the burst of laughter but at least he was smiling for the first time during this visit.

'Maybe he's saving that side of the bed for his cute crew partner. It's not as if you haven't broken a few rules in your time.'

'I think that's my cue to head off as well.' Eddie shook his head. 'Before you two come up with any more ridiculous ideas.' He got to his feet. 'And, just for the record, I'm not planning to share my bed with anyone for the foreseeable future. I've got more than enough going on in my life right now.'

'That makes two of us.' Mick had his eyes closed again. 'Get lost, you two. I'm tired.'

Eddie glanced over his shoulder as he left the room, more worried about his brother now than he had been when he'd arrived. Sure enough, Mick had a hand on his forehead, shading his eyes. From a non-existent bright light? Or was he disguising the fact that he was shedding a tear?

The prickle behind Eddie's own eyes could be blinked away easily enough but the sadness in his heart seemed to be getting bigger. And trying to settle in a little deeper.

It was no wonder an echo of Mick's voice haunted Eddie's sleep that night, but it was something James had said that was foremost in his mind when he arrived at the base the next day to find Jodie with Gus and Alex as they were preparing to move the helicopter out of the hangar and he could hear her laughing at something Gus had said.

He'd seen her smile but this was the first time he'd heard her laugh and he found the corners of his own mouth instantly curving upwards in response—as if he'd heard the joke himself and it had been a particularly good one. It was the first time he'd seen the way genuine mirth could light up Jodie's face as well, and he realised that James had been spot-on.

She really was quite stunning.

It wasn't just her looks. There was an aura about her that was undeniably attractive. She was the kind of person that everybody would gravitate towards at a party—men and women— and it was not necessarily anything to do with sexual attraction.

Her laughter hadn't quite faded when she noticed Eddie approaching so that was another first, to see the way that her eyes could dance when she found something funny. Did they do that when she was happy too? It would be impossible not to feel happy yourself if you were lucky enough to be close enough to see that.

Eddie was feeling better than he had moments

ago, that was for sure. He was still smiling as he headed for the staircase.

'G'day,' he called.

'G'day, mate,' Alex called back, exaggerating an Australian accent.

Gus raised his hand and Jodie nodded in response to his greeting but, if she'd said anything, it was lost in the sound of the giant roller door starting to rattle as it rose to open the hangar and signal the start of a new shift.

A shift that included a mission that took them up the coastline to a beach north of Aberdeen and the view Eddie had from his window was spectacular. The wild surf of the North Sea, dramatic cliffs with occasional ruins of ancient stone castles to be seen and stretches of golden sand between rocky outcrops. A fisherman had slipped on rocks like that and was in trouble with a chest injury that was bad enough for a local ambulance crew, who had reached the injured man via the beach by using a quad bike from a nearby farm, to call for the assistance of the air rescue service. The man had suffered multiple rib fractures and was experiencing increasing respiratory difficulties.

Eddie had two thoughts running through his head as he took a moment to soak in the scenery floating past beneath them. The first was that if Jodie asked him to intubate this patient he'd have to have a very good reason to say no or he might as well kiss goodbye to ever having the kind of relationship he'd want to have with someone he had to work with this closely. He'd seen the look in Jodie's eyes when he'd refused to move and risk losing that protection of their patient's spinal alignment yesterday. Incredulity, that was what it had been. Followed by a sharp dismissal of something that could distract her from doing what needed to be done. She'd avoided direct eye contact after that, which told him she was less than happy, but that had changed when she'd seen him talking to the neurosurgeon in the emergency department in Glasgow.

When he'd told her who Mick was.

The other thought that came from nowhere was something he'd said to his brothers yesterday—that he hadn't realised how much he'd missed his homeland of Scotland. He could feel that bond very strongly right now, with the wildness of the land beneath them. He could almost imagine a lone piper standing on the walls of one of those ruined castles, in the teeth of a freezing wind from the North Sea, perhaps, with the mournful wail of the bagpipes hinting at a breed of stoic people who could face any kind of challenge head-on.

They had their own challenge before they even landed on scene. The fishermen had gone down a cliff track. The local ambulance crew had used a farm bike to travel a considerable distance along the beach. The only way the helicopter could get close, without it taking too long, was to land on the sand between the cliffs and the breaking waves.

'Good thing the tide's still out far enough,' Gus said. 'We've got some nice firm sand to land on. It's on the way in, though, so let's make this as quick as we can.'

Eddie knew not to offer to carry anything Jodie chose to pick up, but he didn't have time, anyway. She had a pack on her back and was out of the aircraft as soon as Alex had opened the door.

By the time they reached the huddle of people at the end of the beach where the sand finished and the rocks began, it was obvious that if they'd taken any longer to get here it would have been too late. The man was struggling to breathe, despite oxygen running at a high flow through the mask he was wearing. They could hear his rasping, dry cough and, even through the plastic of the mask, they could see the blueish tint to his lips. His breathing was too rapid and the monitor the local paramedics had attached was showing a heart rate that was dangerously fast. What was even more concerning was that it was clear that this man's level of consciousness was dropping fast and he knew how much trouble he was in. He looked absolutely terrified.

Jodie crouched beside him. 'We're going to do something to help your breathing and give you something a bit stronger for that pain,' she told him. 'And we're going to take good care of you, okay?'

Eddie could see some of that fear drain from the man's eyes but Jodie might not have noticed because she had her gaze on the disc of her stethoscope as she listened briefly to each side of his chest.

'Breath sounds absent left side,' she said, looking up seconds later. 'There's obvious tracheal deviation and jugular vein distention. Ed, can you draw up some lignocaine and ketamine, please?'

'On it.' He had the drug roll open and reached for the ampoules and a syringe. The paramedics on scene had already gained IV access and had fluids running so it would take very little time to provide the sedation and anaesthetic required to perform the lifesaving procedure of creating an opening in the side of the chest that would save this man's life.

Eddie had seen a finger thoracostomy done many times. He'd done them himself and knew just how careful you had to be with the pressure when you used forceps to open the space between the cut on the skin and the outside of the lung. Not going far enough wouldn't release the air and blood that was caught in the pleural space and creating a lethal pressure that could stop both the lungs and the heart from functioning. Going too far could do damage to the lung or the diaphragm.

He could see how fierce Jodie's concentration was and he was watching her closely enough to see the moment she felt the 'give' of the outer layer of the pleura that was attached to the chest wall. She took the forceps out then, and inserted her finger to do a sweep to ensure that access was enough to release the accumulated air and blood—very carefully, because there was a high risk of injury due to coming into contact with fractured ribs.

Eddie had never seen this procedure done quite this swiftly and effectively but the only indication of satisfaction in a job very well done from Jodie was a single nod. 'I can feel the lung inflating,' she said. 'Can you open a dressing for me, thanks, Ed?'

He already had one in his hand. Alex had the stretcher ready for their patient with the monitoring equipment they would need already switched on and waiting for electrodes, blood pressure cuff and a pulse oximeter to be put in place. They would be ready to take off within a matter of only minutes, so Eddie began packing up their gear as soon as he'd held out the opened package for Jodie to extract the sterile dressing.

She was watching the changes in vital signs that were confirming the success of the procedure. The heart and breathing rates were dropping and the level of circulating oxygen was rising.

But, for a split second, Eddie wasn't looking at anything but Jodie.

It definitely wasn't simply her looks that were stunning.

It wasn't even that aura she had of being more alive than anyone he'd ever met.

Watching her put her skills into action like he'd just witnessed had to be the sexiest thing he'd ever seen.

And okay…nothing was going to happen between them. Not just because of having been warned off by Dion before he'd even met her. Or that Eddie still thought that Jodie didn't like him that much. No…there was something else that was off-putting. He didn't really know what it was, to be honest, but it felt as if something was missing? A small piece of the human jigsaw puzzle that made up Jodie Sinclair but probably not one that mattered, given that getting really close was out of the question. It wasn't something that would stop him being able to be a good colleague with this woman. A friend even, if she'd let him get at least a little closer.

And, oddly, it also didn't seem to be stopping him feeling as if he'd just fallen a little bit in love with her, but it was easy to persuade himself that a first impression could often be a little over the top.

It would wear off soon enough if he ignored it.

There was a punching ball suspended from a rafter in the far corner of the garage of the small house Jodie had inherited from her father. It hadn't been used for a long time, because she preferred to get her exercise by going for a run and using hand weights for a bit of resistance training.

But it was being used tonight and it was remarkably satisfying to be punching it as hard as she could with the protection of her dad's old boxing gloves covering her hands.

It was frustration rather than anger that she needed to deal with.

She wasn't even sure why she was feeling like this, but perhaps that was why the emotion had accumulated to this level over the last couple of weeks that she'd been working with her new partner.

Edward Grisham.

Ed.

Eddie?

No, that felt too familiar. Too...friendly.

Did she want to be friends with Ed?

No.

Yes.

Jodie punched the bag harder and faster. Left, right, left, left right... She could feel perspiration trickling down her spine.

Of course she wanted to be friends with him. Just like she was friends with Gus and Alex and Dion and lots of other people on the air rescue base who were more than just workmates, they were her family.

But there was something different about Edward Grisham.

It wasn't that she didn't trust him. On a professional level she couldn't fault either his skills or his sincerity in the way he cared about his patients. He had a passion for his work and Jodie had worked with enough people in the pre-hospital setting to know that there was something special about Eddie.

That first serious case they'd worked on together, in rescuing that unfortunate mountain biker, was a great example of that. Jodie had rung the spinal unit in Glasgow today to get an update on Caitlin and she'd been delighted to be able to share the good news with the rest of her crew. Caitlin had had successful surgery to stabilise her C5, C6 incomplete fracture and the spinal shock was wearing off to the extent that she had feeling and some movement back in all her limbs. Her consultants were cautiously predicting a much better than expected outcome for her. She might even be able to walk down the aisle unaided for her wedding next year.

Jodie had been watching Eddie when she'd delivered that news. She would have understood completely if his reaction was mixed. Happy for his patient but possibly even a little resentful that his brother hadn't been so lucky? But she hadn't detected anything other than a genuine delight in hearing how well Caitlin was doing.

And who knew how much of that was down to the way Eddie had been so determined to take responsibility for her spinal stability? Ensuring that an incomplete injury didn't become complete due to a secondary injury from an avoidable movement. Not that he was about to take any credit for the part he'd played. Eddie was a team player, wasn't he?

A nice guy.

A nice, highly skilled, intelligent, good-looking guy.

Really, *really* good-looking, with that mop of dark hair and eyes that would be even darker if it wasn't for that glint of whatever it was in them. Amusement? Mischief? *Joie de vivre?*

Jodie hit the punching bag so hard she felt a painful twinge shoot up her arm as far as her shoulder which made her stop. She needed to catch her breath, anyway. She didn't really need to crouch on the floor and press the squashy boxing gloves against her eyes but that was what she did.

To stop herself crying.

Because that was why she couldn't be friends with Eddie.

That attitude to making the most of life in combination with being so *nice*.

It was what she'd loved so much about Joel, wasn't it? What had attracted her to him in the first place. What had come so close, in the end, to utterly destroying her life.

No...

No, no, no...

She wasn't going to get sucked back into that space and she'd had years of practice with how to make sure it didn't happen. Lesson number one: move your body. Not that it was easy to push herself to her feet and get started but that was what Jodie did. And then she ripped off her gloves and kept moving. Straight out of her garage to head for her favourite running route bordering the River Dee through the woodlands towards and around the Inchgarth Reservoir.

The calming hypnosis of her feet drumming

on the pathways and being near water and grass and trees was exactly what she needed to ground herself. Lesson number two: be in the now.

She wasn't going to think about anything to do with the past, like Joel. Like their gap year, when they'd impulsively decided to get married on a tropical island beach. Like their actual wedding day when Joel had been dragged out to sea in a rip. Like that endless, agonising wait for his body to be found and brought back for her to cradle.

She wasn't going to think about the future either. Because, no matter how disturbing it might be, that included Eddie and there was something about him that was dangerous, no matter how solid her belief was that she was never going to get as close to anyone as she had been to Joel.

She would never risk going through a life-destroying loss like that ever again, but Jodie was confident she could maintain the safety barriers she had built so painfully and slowly, piece by piece, putting one foot in front of the other as she tried—and finally succeeded—to move forward and rebuild her life.

Lesson number three: take one day at a time.

CHAPTER FOUR

IT SHOULD HAVE worn off by now.

That attraction that Eddie had been ignoring so effectively that he was quite confident nobody would have guessed that he was so aware of his new crew partner.

Well…not so new, now. How long had he been working at Triple A?

Nearly a month.

Long enough for them to have found a way of working together that was making the reconfiguration of Blue Watch a tight team. The best ever, even, if only that annoying hyperawareness of Jodie would quietly evaporate and he didn't keep finding himself captivated by something like the sound of her voice for the first time that day, or sunlight catching a thread in her hair and making it glow like fire. Even the deft movements of her hands when she was doing something as simple as snapping the head off a drug ampoule and drawing the contents into a syringe could be enough to make it difficult not to let his focus get hijacked.

It was also long enough to wonder whether the medication Mick had been prescribed was actually going to kick in and help him get past this concerning low point in his recovery journey, but that was something else that wasn't yet going quite the way Eddie had been hoping it would. It wasn't helping that it had been a quiet day on base so far, without a single call and far too much time to think. And read.

Eddie clicked out of the medical journal article he'd been reading online because it also wasn't helping to learn that spinal cord injury patients had almost a doubled risk of developing mental health issues, such as depression and anxiety and, not unexpectedly, living with chronic pain was a major factor. Was there something more he could be doing to support Mick? It was all very well to keep telling him to 'hang in there' and that 'things will get better' but, right now, Eddie was beginning to feel like his words were simply platitudes.

He'd had a heart-to-heart with his big sister and brother-in-law about this only a day or two ago when he'd gone out to their gorgeous barn conversion in the countryside just out of Aberdeen. It had been warm enough to sit outside for a barbecue and watch the ducks floating calmly on the pond at the bottom of the garden, which had been a balm all on its own. Ella and Logan's advice had been exactly what he'd needed, as well—which was to look at this period as a stage of grief for everybody involved as they came to terms with and accepted the inevitable changes and losses that Mick would need to adapt to.

'Sometimes,' Logan had told Eddie, 'all you can do is be there for someone and that's all they need you to do. It's their journey and they have to do it at their own pace.'

Ella had stood on tiptoes to fold Eddie into a hug when he was heading home. 'The Mick we all know and love is still in there, I promise. We'll see him back again before too long, I'm sure of it.'

So maybe Eddie was the one who needed to 'hang in there' and give things in his new, rather upside-down, life time to settle properly.

Right now, Eddie was alone in the staffroom. Dion and other admin staff were all occupied in a meeting with city councillors and other officials about an upcoming fundraising event for the air rescue base. Deciding that a breath of fresh air would be a good idea, Eddie took the stairs down into the hangar. He could hear Alex and Jodie, who were busy with some kind of stocktaking in the storeroom and, when he got outside, he found Gus was still pottering around with maintenance chores on his beloved helicopter. Currently he was hosing off the windows and bubble with a spray setting.

'Need some help, Gus?'

'I'm just getting rid of any dust specks so I don't scratch the glass when I'm washing it properly. I'm sure you've got something more interesting to do than cleaning windows.'

'I'm waiting for Dion to finish his meeting. It might be a good time, while it's quiet, to catch him and talk about the boat winch training session he mentioned the other day.'

'Aye… I'd like to talk about that too. But now that you've mentioned the "Q" word, it probably won't happen.' Gus shook his head. 'Grab one of those microfibre cloths and get it wet in that bucket of soapy water and you can help finish this before we get the inevitable call in less than ten minutes. Vertical strokes only, okay?'

'No problem.'

'What are the others up to?'

'Checking expiry dates on some stock. I offered to help but I was told it was a two-person job.' Eddie was leaving a trail of soap bubbles as he pushed the cloth over the windows.

'Gets a bit cosy in that storeroom with more than two people anyway.'

'Yeah…' Eddie gave a huff of sound that was meant to convey relief that he'd dodged a potentially awkward situation but…dammit…there it was again. That prickle of awareness that ran over his skin like a soft breeze at the thought of getting up close and cosy in a restricted space with Jodie Sinclair.

It was a good thing that he was outside with another member of his crew. That the base building was right behind him and behind one of those upper storey windows was Dion's office. What better way to deal with that uncomfortable awareness than to remind himself of the warning he'd been given before he'd even started work here?

'I expect there's a rule or two about that kind of cosy.' He threw a sideways glance at Gus. 'What exactly happened that made Dion warn me that no shenanigans between crew members were going to be tolerated under his watch?'

Gus was still holding the hose, ready to rinse off the soapsuds Eddie was leaving on the acrylic glass.

'That was a couple of years ago. On Red Watch. Mark was the crewman and Zoe was one of the paramedics. They fell for each other and nobody minded but it ended badly. Apparently, Mark cheated on her and they broke up but still had to work together for the rest of that roster and the air was tense enough to cut with a knife. When Mark walked off just before they had to deal with an asthmatic patient who crashed it could have been a disaster. Fortunately, the patient survived but Mark got fired and Zoe resigned because she didn't want to work here even with him gone. It was chaos around here while we covered shifts until we filled the gaps.'

Eddie whistled silently, stooping to get his cloth rinsed and then soapy again. 'That explains a lot. Fair call from Dion, I'd say.'

'At least you don't have any potential shenanigans to worry about, working with Jodie.'

Eddie shook his head, feigning disappointment. 'And there I was, thinking she was starting to like me.'

Gus laughed. 'I'm sure she does. She just likes her job a whole lot better. Lives and breathes it. I reckon she'd convert one of the offices upstairs into a bedroom and live on base if she could get away with it.'

'Really?' Eddie moved onto the bubble at the front of the helicopter, stretching to reach as high as he could. 'Might be a bit of a downer as far as a social life goes.'

'Don't think Jodie's got one,' Gus said. 'Or wants one. I've yet to see her go out with anyone more than once or twice. She was married very young, I believe, and it didn't last long. "Been there, done that," she told me. "Never doing it again." She's happily single and intends to stay that way.'

How intriguing… It seemed like Jodie Sinclair might be a female version of the person that Eddie had been for so many years. The version of himself that he wasn't that impressed with any longer. Maybe she'd had a more valid reason to avoid commitment after a disastrous marriage and Eddie might be moving on to a more settled lifestyle but his memories of so many good times could still make him smile.

'She's a girl after my own heart,' he said.

'Just as well Dion told you the score then.' Gus turned the hose back on and Eddie stood back, dropping his cloth into the bucket. 'Crew members are off-limits.'

'No worries,' Eddie assured him. Then he grinned. 'You're quite safe, mate.'

He had to duck as a spray of water came in his direction. They were both still laughing as their pagers went off but then Gus shook his head.

'How long was that? Eight minutes?'

''Bout that.' But Eddie was still smiling. He knew Gus was just as happy as he was to get the callout. This was what they were all here for. Stocktaking and washing helicopters was just marking time between the opportunities to provide the best possible care for sick and injured people in that vital space of time before they could get to the emergency department of a well-equipped hospital.

It was only a short flight this time.

A thirty-four-year-old farmer, Dylan McKenzie, in an area only fifteen minutes' flight time north of Aberdeen, had apparently been gored and trampled by one of his Highland cattle. Local first responders and the police were in attendance, currently working on controlling an arterial bleed.

The cattle, and their calves, had been cleared from the field and there was plenty of room for Gus to bring the helicopter down not far from where a police vehicle was parked on the grass. They had arrived before the ambulance that had been dispatched from the nearest station by road.

The first responders were doing their best but the dressing over a wound they were applying pressure to was blood soaked and the young farmer's skin was a nasty shade of grey that Eddie knew was an ominous sign of potential haemorrhagic shock from massive blood loss. He was also agitated, which was another sign that his brain wasn't receiving enough oxygen.

'Someone needs to look after my wife…' was the first thing he said, between gasps of pain, as Jodie crouched beside him. '… Debbie… She's pregnant…'

Eddie had already noticed the young woman who looked to be in the late stages of pregnancy. She was standing beside the police car and had a small boy who was clutching her legs and sobbing. A policewoman had her arm around the young mother's shoulders.

'She's being taken care of,' Jodie calmly assured Dylan. 'It's my job to take care of you and I've got Eddie and Alex with me. I'm just going to put a mask over your face so we can give you some oxygen, is that okay?'

But Dylan was shaking his head. 'They didn't mean to hurt me,' he said. 'It's because…they were trying to protect their calves. *Oh*…help me…please…'

He sounded in extreme pain and increasingly short of breath. Eddie opened a pouch on the side of the defibrillator and took out the SpO2 monitor. He put it on Dylan's finger and then nodded at the first responder, a middle-aged man wearing overalls that advertised his job as a mechanic with a local garage.

'You've done a good job, mate,' he said. 'Can I take over from you there?'

'Please…'

Eddie lifted the dressing to find an ongoing pulsatile blood loss. He folded a gauze square and used it, with his finger, to apply a very direct pressure to the bleeding vessel because the pressure that had been put on so far had been too diffuse to allow a clot to form and block the damaged artery.

Alex was cutting the thick woollen jumper and shirt underneath to expose Dylan's chest and Jodie was watching the chest wall movements as she fitted her stethoscope to her ears and then put the disc onto skin as she listened to his breath sounds. Eddie had seen the severe bruising already appearing on one side of the chest which told him that they could probably add fractured ribs to the list of injuries.

There was so much that needed to be done in the shortest possible time to try and stabilise this patient before they could move him.

'Alex, can you grab a CAT tourniquet for me, please?'

'Sure.'

'And I need a non-rebreather mask and the oxygen cylinder, thanks, Alex.' Jodie glanced up at Eddie. 'Breath sounds equal. Respiratory rate thirty-six. Heart rate around one forty.'

Eddie acknowledged the information with a nod. The higher-than-normal vital signs for heart and breathing rates fitted the picture of haemorrhagic shock and if they were going to save this patient they had to try and stop any further blood loss and replace volume. He slipped the strap of the Combat Application Tourniquet through the buckle and pulled it tight before fastening it. Then he twisted the plastic rod until the bleeding from the gash in his arm was finally stopped.

Jodie was on the side of Dylan's uninjured arm, holding his wrist, but the quick shake of her head told Eddie that there was no palpable radial pulse. Trying to gain peripheral IV access was only going to waste time and it was imperative that it happened quickly. It wasn't just to provide pain relief, replace fluid volume and infuse the blood products they carried in the helicopter that Alex had just been sent to fetch. There were also drugs that needed IV administration, like TXA that could help stop the bleeding by influencing the clotting process and others that could cause constriction of veins to help keep blood volume in vital organs or help the heart pump harder to move what blood remained through the body.

'I'm going to cannulate the external jugular,' Jodie told Eddie. 'And we might get a second line in via an intraosseous access.'

An ambulance pulled into the field as Eddie was doing a body sweep to make sure they weren't missing any other obvious injuries that were contributing to blood loss and someone else, possibly a relative, arrived to take the small boy away from the scene. Eddie ran his hands down Dylan's side, into the gap beneath his lower spine and down each leg, but there was no blood to be seen on his gloves. What he did find, however, made his heart sink.

The cry of pain from Dylan when he'd touched his hips and lower back made him gently palpate both iliac crests above each hip.

'Pelvic instability,' he informed Jodie quietly.

She glanced up for a split second, from where she was unrolling a kit that contained everything she needed to insert a wide bore cannula into the large vein on the side of Dylan's neck. The eye contact was so brief it almost didn't happen, but it still conveyed how much of a challenge they were up against. If Dylan was losing blood internally due to a serious pelvic fracture on top of the amount he'd already lost from an external arterial bleed, they could well be fighting a losing battle.

If anything, that knowledge only made them fight harder. This was a young farmer. A husband. A father. His distraught wife was watching the efforts to save Dylan but probably couldn't see very much with another ambulance crew and more emergency responders crowded around and trying to assist by holding up bags of IV fluid and blood, supplying equipment, drawing up drugs and finding blankets to try and keep Dylan warm. It was probably just as well she couldn't see too much as Dylan slipped into unconsciousness and then cardiac arrest but Eddie liked that Jodie was using one of the extra medics to keep his wife informed at every step about what was being done to try and save her husband.

Her skill in leading a large team of people was something he hadn't seen before and Jodie was as capable in this tense scenario as in everything else she did, but, sadly, in the end there was nothing more they could do. Dylan was still losing blood faster than they could replace it and so, when he went into cardiac arrest, there was simply not enough blood volume for the heart to be able to pump. As lead medic, it was Jodie's call to stop the resuscitation attempt and it was impossible not to notice how calm her voice was when she made the decision.

'I'm calling it,' she said. She glanced at her watch. 'Time of death fifteen forty-three hours.'

Her face was expressionless as she got to her feet, turned away from the patient they'd been working on so desperately hard for what seemed like for ever but had probably been no more than about forty-five minutes, and walked towards where Dylan's wife, Debbie, was still standing beside a police car. He couldn't look away as he watched the two women—Jodie standing so upright but Debbie crumpling as she received the news, despite knowing it was coming. He saw Jodie reach out but there were other people closer who could catch the devastated woman and care for her.

Perhaps it was only Eddie who saw that Jodie's fingers clenched into a tight ball as she turned away. That her face was so rigid it was obvious that she was struggling to keep her composure. Then, she seemed to take a deeper breath and regain control. By the time she noticed Eddie watching her she was close enough for him to see that she was focused on what needed to happen next.

And, of course, she knew exactly what the protocols were for a situation like this.

'There's a standardised post-resuscitation procedure for all unexpected adult deaths in the community, that you might not have caught up with yet?'

'No, sorry. I haven't seen that yet.'

'The main thing we need to be aware of is that when attempts have been made to resuscitate the patient and the death has been confirmed at the scene, we need to leave everything in place— the ET tube, cannulas, ECG electrodes et cetera. It's up to the police and the SFIU—the Scottish Fatalities Investigation Unit to organise the next steps and remove the body because this now becomes an investigation of a sudden death in the community. Could you explain that to the relatives, please, Ed? The wife might be a bit shocked to have us just pack up and disappear.'

'Of course.'

Eddie was still watching Jodie like a hawk but he couldn't detect any other signs that she wasn't totally in control. He could, in fact, almost *feel* the barriers that had gone up with the distance being created by a man with a name suddenly becoming 'the body' and the distraught mother of his children, who had to be about the same age as Jodie, becoming simply 'the wife'.

But Eddie had seen behind the mask, hadn't he?

Just for a blink of time, but it had been long enough to realise what it was that had been niggling at the back of his mind. What that 'something' was that had felt as if it was missing.

Empathy?

An emotional connection with her patients?

It wasn't that it wasn't there. It was that Jodie chose not to let it show. Or maybe she didn't even want to acknowledge it herself.

And Eddie wanted to know why.

She didn't want to.

She tried not to.

But Jodie couldn't stop that glance from the window as the helicopter rose straight up from the scene until they were high enough for Gus to turn them towards home. She knew what she would see. All unnecessary people had been cleared from the area as police tape was put up to secure the scene. The wash from the helicopter rotors was blowing some of the debris of packaging away from the still figure of the young father but that was evidence as well and someone else would be responsible for cleaning it up at a later point.

They had protected Dylan's dignity as much as possible, leaving a pillow under his head and covering him with a blanket. His wife was the only person near him as the air rescue crew finally departed. She was kneeling and leaning over Dylan as best she could with her pregnant belly, and maybe it was Jodie's imagination but, even at this height, she thought she could see Debbie's shoulders shaking with her agonised sobbing.

The way she'd knelt over Joel's body that day…? Would Debbie also try and hold her husband the way she'd held Joel—as if her own body warmth could somehow breathe life back into him?

Ohh... That pain didn't often surface these days, but when it did, it was still more than sharp enough to cause real pain.

Jodie shifted her gaze, being careful not to look in Eddie's direction or say anything that might spark conversation between any of the crew. She flipped over her tablet in its almost bombproof casing and tapped it into life. Paper-work for any patient could be detailed but for a case like this, that would automatically be part of a wider investigation, the reporting had to be immaculate. She didn't want the distraction of anyone talking to her. Or even looking at her.

Especially Eddie.

Because Jodie had the horrible feeling that he'd noticed the way she'd had to hang on to her control a little more tightly than usual, after having to remove any last shred of hope that she knew Debbie would have been clinging on to that they were going to be able to save her husband and the father of her child and unborn baby. She also knew what Debbie was about to face and how hard it was going to be to survive that tsunami of grief.

The sooner this job was over and done with, the better. It was a good thing that by the time they'd sorted out the mess their gear was in and restocked depleted kits it would be past the end of their shift and she could go home. And then she could run and run and run, until the ground—and the foundations of her life—felt completely stable again.

Alex and Gus focused on what needed to be done inside the helicopter when they were back on base. Eddie and Jodie opened their kits on the floor of the storeroom and found everything they needed to replenish supplies. The drug roll was the last task to be done. Gus and Alex had already brought the helicopter back into the hangar. They poked their heads into the storeroom.

'Need a hand?' Alex asked.

'No, we're all good,' Eddie told them. 'We'll be done soon.'

'We're heading into the Pig and Thistle for a quick beer before we go home,' Gus said as he turned away. 'Maybe you'd like to join us?'

Eddie was already familiar with the nearest pub to the base, which also happened to be very close to the apartment he'd taken over from the paramedic whose position he'd filled. He was also a big fan of having an informal debrief to tackle the emotional aftermath of a case like they'd just had, but this time he shook his head regretfully.

'I'm visiting my brother,' he told them. 'I promised I'd arrive with some fish and chips for his dinner. It was always his favourite Friday night takeaway when we were kids.'

Not that Mick was likely to do more than taste it, but Eddie wasn't about to break his promise.

'Next time, then,' Alex excused him. 'Jodie?'

'I'll see how I go when I'm done with the paperwork.'

'Okay…no pressure…'

It took another fifteen minutes to go through the raft of drugs they'd used in Dylan's attempted resuscitation and everything had to be recorded and signed for by both of them in the drug register.

'I've got the last one.' Eddie held up two glass ampoules. 'Tranexamic acid, five hundred milligrams in five mils, solution for injection.' He held out the ampoules for Jodie to double check. 'Expiry date next year.'

He slotted the ampoules into the drug kit while Jodie was recording the details. She signed the column and then held out the pen.

'Your turn.'

Eddie scribbled his signature and then closed the book. 'So…you heading to the pub with the others, then?'

'I don't think so.' Jodie took the book and slotted it back on a shelf.

'How come?'

The query slipped out before Eddie had given it any thought. He knew instantly that he'd made a mistake as Jodie turned and gave him a glance sharp enough to cut paper. Her tone was just as cutting.

'Maybe I don't want to. Does it matter? Is it actually any of your business?'

Whoa…

Eddie held her gaze. He could take this the wrong way and back off, but he knew that if he took the easy way out of this suddenly intense moment he'd never get the chance to find out why Jodie was so good at hiding.

Which was what she was doing now. Hiding from his question. Hiding from him. Hiding from the other people she had worked with long enough for them to know not to put any pressure on personal boundaries.

Eddie got it.

And perhaps he got rather more than Jodie might think he got. Because he'd had the wake-up call of a family crisis and could look back on the way he'd been living his life as a way of hiding from the stuff that really mattered. Like committing to relationships in a way that actually meant something.

He wasn't about to put any pressure on her either, but he wanted Jodie to know that if he had seen behind her mask she could trust him not to use it against her or even mention it.

That she could trust *him*.

Maybe his lips curved just a little, but it was Eddie's eyes doing most of the smiling and Jodie caught her bottom lip between her teeth.

'Sorry,' she muttered. 'I didn't mean that to sound so…erm…'

'I know.'

Eddie was still holding her gaze. Or maybe Jodie was holding his. Maybe it didn't matter because something bigger was holding them both. The air in this small room, with its shelves so tightly packed with medical supplies and the heavy security door firmly closed, seemed to be getting heavier. Pressing down on them.

Pushing them closer together.

Neither of them said a word. They didn't seem to need to. By whatever means, whether it was body language or telepathy, apparently the desire was expressed, permission sought—and granted.

Jodie slowly came up onto her tiptoes. Eddie bent his head just as slowly, turning it in the last moments, just before he closed his eyes and finally broke that contact, so that his lips were at the perfect angle to cover Jodie's with a soft, lingering touch.

When he lifted his head, he found Jodie's eyes were open before his. Maybe she hadn't closed them at all? Because of their soft, chocolate brown colour, he could also see that her pupils were getting bigger fast enough to tell him that she had liked that kiss as much as he did. That quick intake of her breath suggested that she wanted more.

Eddie had played this game often enough to be an expert. He knew there was an easy way to find out...

This time, the kiss wasn't nearly as soft and her lips parted beneath his, her tongue meeting his almost instantly.

Oh, yeah...

She wanted more.

So did Eddie. But not here. Not now. Not just because they'd be breaking all sorts of rules and it was a bad idea, anyway. No...he had a promise to keep to someone else and Edward Grisham never broke a promise.

He broke the kiss, instead.

'I have to go,' he said.

Jodie's gaze slid away from his. 'Me too. We're done here.'

But Eddie was smiling as he turned away. He spoke softly but he knew that Jodie would be able to hear him perfectly well.

'I'm not so sure about that,' he said.

CHAPTER FIVE

IT WAS STILL THERE.

The memory of that kiss.

How long had it been since Jodie had experienced a kiss that had the ability to make time stop like that? One that even an echo of it, in the form of a memory, was guaranteed to generate that kind of delicious sensation, like the anticipation of experiencing something you wanted more than anything else in the world, deep in her belly?

Was it too long, or was it not long enough…?

Maybe the really disturbing thought was that the memory was more than simply about that physical touch of lips on lips and the unspoken conversation that it had evoked. It was about what had led up to that kiss.

That gruelling case when a young man, the love of someone's life, the father of a child who was too young to understand that his life was about to be changed for ever and another who hadn't even taken a first breath, had been ripped away from the world and, despite the best training, the best equipment and enough experience to know exactly what they needed to do, she and Eddie had been helpless to prevent it happening. Keeping enough of an emotional distance from the heartbreak that went way too close to the bone because it was so personal had been so much harder than usual. She'd had to fight hard and Jodie had even wondered if Eddie might have witnessed that hidden struggle.

Had he seen something she'd thought she had been successful in hiding from anyone for so long she didn't even consider it to be an issue these days? It was the last thing Jodie would have wanted to happen but, at least if he had, he had also made it clear that he wasn't about to pry too far into her personal life. She'd bitten his head off, mind you, when he'd asked why she might not want to join in a happy hour at the local pub, but he hadn't been offended. Quite the opposite? The look he'd given her made her think he might understand far more than she might be comfortable with, but it had also made her begin to feel, deep down in her bones, that she could trust him.

And how powerful had *that* feeling been?

Powerful enough that, when combined with the stress they had both experienced that day and what it was about this newcomer in her life that was so damned attractive, it had probably made that kiss inevitable. On her side, anyway.

That Eddie had responded the way he did—almost as if he'd expected the opportunity to arise and had been looking forward to it—had ignited something that Jodie wasn't ready to acknowledge. Not that there was any point in even thinking about it. No matter how attractive they might find each other, going any further down that track was not going to happen.

You didn't mess around with your crewmates and that was that.

End of story.

Except it was still there.

Nobody else knew it was there, of course. Eddie was so good at hiding it that Jodie might have wondered if it was actually there herself in the days following that unfortunate lapse of good judgement in the storeroom that night.

But the occasional eye contact that was held for just a heartbeat too long, that gave her an unmistakable frisson of a sensation she preferred not to analyse too deeply, was a dead giveaway. So were those touches of physical contact that was inevitable when you were working so closely with someone—taking a drug ampoule from their hand to double check the name, dosage and expiry date, for example. Or holding a limb so that a splint or dressing could be applied with minimal discomfort.

Maybe Eddie wasn't feeling it as much as she was and that was why it was so easy for him to carry on as though nothing had happened?

As the days passed and Jodie relaxed enough to step back from what had, after all, been no more than a momentary blip in what was becoming a good professional relationship, she could see a gleam in Eddie's gaze occasionally that was definitely an acknowledgment that they had stepped, briefly, into a very different space. One that they both knew was simply not acceptable amongst crew members and could, in fact, get them both into a lot of trouble, but that gleam suggested that Eddie had no regrets. That, perhaps, he liked the fact that it was a secret between them?

Whatever. What had impressed Jodie was that he was so good at keeping that secret. Instinct told her that she could trust him to keep on keeping it, which was strengthening the impression that she could trust him on a personal as well as a professional level. And wasn't that the basis for a friendship that could grow into the kind of bond she had with the other people on this air rescue base that she considered to be her family? And, if she was really honest with herself, that buzz of sensation that she knew perfectly well was all about an unusually strong sexual attraction was not exactly an unpleasant thing to be experiencing occasionally.

It made her feel distinctly more alive—where every sense became heightened to the point that colours were brighter and food tasted better and you could feel things with a much keener awareness. It was kind of similar to the heightened awareness and the ability to think and move faster that came with the rush of adrenaline associated with the more dangerous challenges one could face working on a frontline helicopter rescue crew. Challenges like rescues at sea, which could mean that a medic needed to be lowered to the deck of a moving vessel or dropped into a rough sea to reach a person in the water. The sort of missions that didn't happen often and were more likely to occur in unpredictable conditions, so regular training sessions were vital to keep skills as sharp as needed for when an emergency like that presented itself and there were lives at stake for both the rescuers and those in trouble.

Jodie and her crewmates were gathering in the meeting room upstairs at the base, early on the morning of a day they weren't on duty. Was that why it looked as though Eddie hadn't bothered shaving this morning? Jodie had to stop herself taking another look at the shadow on his jawline so she didn't get distracted by wondering how that faint stubble might feel beneath her fingers.

Or against her skin…?

Dion had an image projected onto a whiteboard at the front of the meeting room and Jodie deliberately focused on the chart of numbers and letters.

'Here's the marine shipping forecast for the Cromarty area,' Dion told them. 'And it looks like we couldn't have ordered up a better day for this training session.' He pointed to a column of figures. 'There's a light breeze with a wind speed of six knots, gusting to nine. Cloud cover of twenty percent with no rain expected and a swell of less than a metre, lasting six to seven seconds.'

'Nice…' Alex was looking happy. 'Is the coastguard rescue team good to go?'

'They've already been out in their all-weather lifeboat doing some training of their own with a couple of new volunteers. They're expecting us on scene in forty minutes, so you'd better get your skates on and get into your wetsuits. You'll do the Hi-Line exercises first with the coastguard rescue team, but they'll stay on scene for the rest of the session when you're doing the person in the water retrieval.' Dion was smiling at them all. 'Stay safe,' he said. 'And have fun…'

* * *

Oh…*man*…

Seeing Jodie Sinclair encased in that skin-tight black wetsuit, that didn't leave very much at all to the imagination with regard to every curve of her body, had to be the sexiest thing Eddie had ever seen. He found himself needing to take a deep breath and stop himself taking yet another glance. He followed Alex's example instead, and watched the sea beneath them as they became airborne and headed straight offshore.

It was a brief period of time between their preparations and arriving at the designated area for the training exercise and staring at a relatively smooth patch of the North Sea wasn't enough to stop Eddie's mind from going where it was determined to go.

Back to that kiss…

Yet again…

He knew it wasn't going to be repeated. It shouldn't have happened in the first place, and the last thing Eddie wanted was to even suggest breaking rules that could end up with disciplinary action against Jodie and, worse, him being transferred to another crew or even fired but… but knowing all that didn't seem to be enough to let him just forget about it.

On the contrary, the idea of a secret, *illicit* liaison with Jodie was taking that level of desire to a whole new, unbelievable notch. Which, in a way, was a good thing because Eddie knew that reality could never live up to an expectation like that, except in fantasies. And sexual fantasies would never encroach on his mind during working hours. Ever.

He knew it wouldn't be at all surprising if he found himself thinking about Jodie in that wetsuit when he was alone in his bed in that tiny basement flat later tonight, mind you...

Spotting the bright orange paintwork of the coastguard vessel below them made it easy to flick any personal thoughts from his mind. He raised his hand to point it out to the others but they'd already seen the boat.

'Target sighted,' Alex said. 'One o'clock.'

'Roger that.' Gus was establishing contact with the boat crew as he got the helicopter into a position and speed that would keep them at a steady distance behind the vessel. The boat crew were well trained in this exercise but Gus still went through every step with them again.

'The Hi-Line will be lowered. Take hold of the weighted end and take in the slack, coiling the line onto the deck. Do not attach the Hi-Line to any part of the vessel, is that understood?'

'Loud and clear,' came the response.

Alex was leaning out of the open door of the helicopter, his hand on the line as it was lowered towards the boat, and Eddie was also watching it carefully. This type of boat didn't present as many problems as a yacht with its mast and rigging would but they still had to be sure the 'heaving in' or Hi-Line didn't snag on anything.

They paid the line out again as Gus dropped the helicopter's position further behind the boat and then it was Jodie's turn to be winched down first. The line that the two deck crew on the coastguard boat were holding was still attached to the winch hook and, as she was lowered, Eddie was watching the Hi-Line even more carefully now. The crew on the boat had to haul the line in to keep the correct tension that would stop Jodie being spun by the rotor wash or the lines dropping into the sea or getting caught on anything. He was holding his breath as he watched her getting close enough to get pulled onboard the boat, detach the winch hook and signal to have it raised.

The process was reversed to take Jodie off the boat and lift her back into the helicopter and then crew members both in the air and on board the boat swapped places so that others could get the hands-on experience that exercises like this provided so well. It was Eddie's turn to be winched down and it went as smoothly as he had expected. Too easy. He'd done some pretty hairy rescue missions in the dark, in much bigger seas than this in Australia but it was always good to refresh the skills, especially when working with a new crew.

Gus moved the helicopter a little further away from the coastguard vessel for the second part of their refresher training. Both Jodie and Eddie needed flippers, masks and snorkels in addition to the lifejackets over their wetsuits for this part of the exercise.

'Who's going to be our victim for the first run?' he asked. 'Jodie?'

'Fine by me.' She pushed her foot into the second, bright orange flipper. 'Could do with a dip.'

The sea conditions might be ideal, with a rescue boat not far away, but there was still something a bit scary about being dropped into the ocean.

Well…not dropped, exactly. Jodie couldn't say anything around the mouthpiece of her snorkel. She couldn't hear anything either, because she couldn't wear her usual helmet with its inbuilt sound technology in the water, but she could see Alex's lips moving and knew exactly what his calm voice would sound like as he went through his own protocol and patter with Gus after being cleared to open the door and then attach the winch hook to Jodie's harness.

'Moving Jodie to door. Clear skids.'

'Clear skids,' Gus would say if he was happy for the winch to proceed in these conditions.

'Clear to winch out?'

'Clear to winch.'

Jodie could see the skids passing her line of sight as she dropped beneath the helicopter. She could see the grey swells of sea water coming rapidly closer.

Alex would let the others know what was happening by counting down the metres as she got closer to entering the water.

Jodie didn't look up but she knew Alex would be leaning out, safely anchored by his own strop, watching her every move. She couldn't look up, anyway, because she was busy opening the carabiner that had kept her attached to the winch hook. She took it off and then held it out and up so that Alex could see it clearly and know that it was safe to retrieve the hook back onboard.

She glanced up to see the hook swinging as it was quickly wound back up. Eddie would be getting ready to be winched down now and he would be carrying an extra harness for her. Jodie's job was simply to float in the water, being the patient. Someone who'd been caught in a rip and swept out to sea, perhaps. Or a survivor from a yacht that had caught fire or been sunk by a collision or bad weather. She always welcomed the opportunity to see what she did for a job from the point of view of the person who was being rescued but, as she rode the swell in the chill of the ocean water around her, she could sense something more this time.

Because it was Eddie that she could see waiting on the skid of the hovering helicopter for the okay to be winched down to rescue her.

Jodie was someone who was firmly anchored in reality and never willingly conjured up any kind of fantasy situation unless it was a patient scenario or some other kind of simulation that could improve her skills—like learning to escape from a helicopter when it had crashed into water, for example, so it was more than a little disconcerting to find herself suddenly imagining what it would be like to be in real danger. To have Edward Grisham swooping in like a knight in shining armour, albeit dressed in a wetsuit and unrecognisable with his head covering, mask and snorkel on. To feel him holding her and keeping her safe as they were both lifted out of that danger.

Oh, my...

Jodie could see that Eddie was entering the water now, not far away from her. She raised both her arms in a signal for help and was ready to get the harness in place and be hooked onto the winch hook still attached to Eddie. He held his arm straight up to let Alex know they were ready to be winched up and Jodie could feel the drag of the water as she was pulled clear.

Now she could really feel what it was like to be this close to this man's body and it was, quite literally, stealing her breath away. Because she already knew what it was like to be kissed by him? Because there was genuinely an element of danger in what they were doing so her senses were already maxed out? Maybe it had something to do with the rush of external air pressure from the helicopter's rotors or it might have been the combination of all those factors. It was no time at all, really, before she was safely back inside the cabin and could breathe again but… something had changed, hadn't it?

Something had escaped from the place it had been so very carefully confined for a very long time.

And Jodie wasn't at all sure what she should do about that.

Everything that had been in touch with, soaked in or splashed by salt water had to be thoroughly cleaned after the training exercises were finished. Gus and Alex took care of helicopter surfaces and winch gear like harnesses and strops but Eddie and Jodie were responsible for all the items they'd used themselves. Rinsing the likes of masks and snorkels was an easy enough task but the most time-consuming chore was getting out of their wetsuits, having a hot shower to warm up properly and then washing the suits.

There was a tub plumbed onto the outside of the hangar near the storeroom and a line to hang the suits on after they were washed. Eddie was opening all the zips on the suits and turning them inside out as Jodie filled the large tub with cool water and added the liquid cleaning product.

Alex appeared around the side of the hangar. 'We're done with the chopper and putting it away. Do you guys need a hand?'

'Nah…we're good, thanks,' Eddie responded. 'Thanks for today, mate. Reckon it's my turn to shout you and Gus a round at the Pig and Thistle this time if you don't mind waiting a wee while so that we can finish our housework here.'

But Alex shook his head. 'Gus is taking his family out to dinner tonight for a birthday celebration and… I've got a date.' The way the young crewman ducked his head suggested that this was both a new relationship and potentially promising.

'Ooh…' Jodie was grinning. 'Bring her along. I'll let you know her suitability rating later.'

'I'm not sure she's ready to meet you lot yet, but if she's brave enough we'll drop in. Not that I'm going to take any notice whatsoever of your suitability score.' Alex might be grinning back at her but he shook his head even more firmly as he turned to walk away. 'You might want to take a look at your own love life before you start offering advice to others, my friend.'

'I'm perfectly happy with my love life exactly the way it is, thank you.' Jodie took the wetsuits from Eddie and plunged them into the water. 'Can you get the masks and snorkels dry and put them away while I do this? And did you find where the flippers ended up?'

'Yeah… Alex had already put them away.' Eddie picked up the masks. 'Do you think he'll bring his date to the pub?'

'Doubt it.' Jodie laughed. 'We're probably far too intimidating.'

'Do you still want to go?'

Jodie seemed to be focused on kneading the wetsuit fabric to make sure the cleaner was doing its job. 'Sure…why not? I think we've earned a bit of down time, don't you? And the Pig and Thistle does some amazing potato skins. Don't know about you, but I'm starving after all that exercise and sea air.'

Jodie's casual question was still hanging in the air as Eddie headed for the cupboard where the wetsuits would hang once dry again. There was a rack for flippers of various sizes and the other accessories needed for sea missions.

Why not, indeed?

Because if nobody else turned up, it might feel like a date?

No. He pushed that unhelpful thought aside. This was, in fact, a perfect opportunity to do what colleagues should be able to do without even blinking—share a drink after a good day of working or training together.

It might even be a step closer to friendship?

Oh, help…what had she been thinking?

She'd had the chance to get out of this when they'd discovered Gus was busy and Alex unlikely to bring his new girlfriend for a drink with his workmates but she'd been the one to say she'd like to go anyway. Because they'd earned it and because she liked the crispy, deep-fried potato skins that arrived too hot to pick up instantly, covered with a generous sprinkling of sea salt crystals and grated Parmesan cheese.

So, here they were with a basket of potato skins in front of them, along with tall glasses of her favourite lager and… Eddie looked gorgeous in his faded old jeans and a ribbed black fisherman's jumper with the sleeves pushed up and his hair all rumpled and even more of a five o'clock shadow than he'd had this morning and…

And it suddenly felt like a *date*…

What was even worse was that that occasional

pleasant buzz of sexual attraction had become a steady hum that was increasing in intensity and impossible to ignore. Maybe talking about work would help?

'So…have you ever done a sea rescue for real?'

Eddie nodded. 'Quite a few,' he added, before taking a big bite of the crunchy potato snack. 'I worked on the coast of Australia. There's a lot that happens at sea.'

Jodie picked up a potato skin for herself, which was as delicious as they always were, but she was watching Eddie from the corner of her eye as he finished his and then sucked some grains of salt and cheese fragments from his fingertips. That hum of sensation in her belly was split in half by a spear of what could only be deemed sheer lust.

Thank goodness he started speaking then, because Jodie would have been incapable of saying anything.

'Had three guys in a lifeboat once. Big seas. The mast on their yacht had snapped and it overturned. The swells were big enough for the inflatable lifeboat to disappear between them and it was in the middle of the night and raining. The wind was enough to have me swinging like a pendulum.'

Jodie's jaw was dropping, her food forgotten. 'Sounds terrifying.'

Eddie could have made himself sound like a real hero by denying that but, instead, his face sobered as he held her gaze.

'It was,' he said quietly. 'I was in the water and swam to the boat and the two guys that were still conscious insisted I take their mate first because he was the worst off, but I could see they were all in trouble. I was supposed to swap with my crew partner for the next retrieval but it was going to take too long so I just went down again myself. Twice. Getting them on board ASAP was the best we could do for them. They were dangerously hypothermic.'

'And the first guy?'

'I kind of knew I was winching a body by the time I had him in the harness.' Eddie shook his head. 'But I could have been wrong and, in the end, I was glad we took him home. His family were very grateful to get him back. They came to see me, after the funeral. To tell me how much it meant to them. To thank us.'

Jodie could see the muscles in his jaw and throat moving as he swallowed hard. As if he was holding back tears?

'Sometimes,' he added softly, 'there are moments in this job that make you feel very humble, aren't there?'

There were. But some people never felt like that because it took a level of compassion and humanity that wasn't a given, even in a profession that was all about helping other people. It was also rare to find a man who was okay with not only feeling but sharing something that emotional.

Jodie couldn't look away from Eddie.

He wasn't looking away from her either.

And it was like that moment in the storeroom, before that kiss, only it was ten times more intense.

It was Eddie who broke the bubble of silence they were in, in the middle of a crowded, noisy pub. His words were so quiet Jodie shouldn't have been able to hear them as clearly as she could.

'I think I want to kiss you again,' he murmured.

It was Jodie's turn to swallow hard.

'I think I want you to,' she said.

'We work together. We can't do that.'

'No…' Jodie felt the need to dampen her lips with the tip of her tongue and she could actually feel the intensity go up a big notch as Eddie's gaze dropped from her eyes to watch her mouth. 'But…have you ever…?'

'Yeah…'

'Did anyone find out?'

'No…'

The quirk of Eddie's eyebrow suggested that

an encounter could be all the more desirable because it was against the rules. She could believe that. Jodie dragged her gaze away from his face. She could see the basket of potato skins sitting there, getting rapidly colder, but she wasn't hungry any longer. Not for food, anyway.

'I don't do relationships,' she told Eddie without looking at him. She would never lead anyone on, nor allow them to expect something she was not prepared to give.

'Neither do I,' he said.

Aye…she could believe that too. Someone like Eddie would have any number of women throwing themselves at him. Living a life of casual encounters or a series of 'friendships with benefits' certainly fitted the initial impression of him as being a maverick. She might have been wrong about that on a professional basis but it could still well apply to his personal life.

And if there were none of the expectations that came with a relationship, wouldn't that mean the possibility of conflict would also be non-existent? That was why the Mark and Zoe incident had been such an issue, wasn't it? Why it was understandable that Dion had made it so clear it was not to happen again on the Aberdeen Air Ambulance base.

But what she and Eddie were—sort of—discussing was no more than a hook-up. A mutual decision as adults who wouldn't be hurting anyone else by giving in to a sexual chemistry they happened to have discovered with each other.

Jodie released her bottom lip from where it had been caught between her teeth. Somehow, she managed to keep her tone perfectly casual. Matter-of-fact, even.

'It *is* kind of distracting, working with someone that you find attractive,' she said.

'It is.' Eddie cleared his throat. 'Maybe it's something we just need to get out of our systems?'

'You mean…' Jodie couldn't finish her sentence. Her mouth was getting dry. She reached for her glass and took a mouthful of the cool lager. Then she raised her gaze to meet Eddie's. 'Are you saying we should do something about it?'

'I'm saying it's an option. Might let us get past the distraction and be able to move on.'

The thought that Eddie might have been thinking about that kiss as much as she had only added to an intensity that was about to spiral out of control. Jodie knew she was playing with fire because there were things about this man that reminded her of Joel—the love of her life that she had no intention of even trying to replace. Ever.

But, in a way, that was also her safety net. Because it meant that she'd never fall in love with

Eddie. Or anyone else. This was purely about sexual attraction and it wasn't as if she'd denied herself the occasional indulgence in what was a basic need, after all. And perhaps once would be enough. To satisfy her curiosity.

To satisfy a level of want that was becoming almost unbearable...

Her word was only a whisper. 'Where?'

'My place is just around the corner.'

Jodie pulled in a slow breath. Her gaze drifted towards the food and drinks they'd ordered. 'You don't want to finish any of this?'

'No.' Eddie's chair scraped on wooden floor-boards. He held out his hand to help her to her feet and then leaned closer so that his lips brushed her ear. 'I want *you*, Jodie...'

CHAPTER SIX

HIS APARTMENT.

His bed.

His...epiphany?

Who knew sex could be like this? This much fun but, at the same time, feel like something so much more than simply *fun*?

Something genuinely funny covered those awkward moments of getting naked with someone for the very first time because, in Eddie's haste to peel Jodie's tee shirt from her body, it somehow rolled itself up and made the armhole too small to let her get her arm out. They were both weak with laughter by the time they had unravelled the fabric and removed the garment.

But then, as Eddie dropped the tee shirt onto the floor and stood there looking down at Jodie wearing nothing more than her bra and knickers, the enormity struck him of doing this—the most intimate of touching—for the very first time with someone new. With an almost reverent movement, he lifted Jodie's chin with a gentle forefinger and bent his head to kiss her.

Softly.

It felt as if he was making a promise to respect this. To respect *her*. And to remind her that she could trust him.

And then sheer need took over and broke any remaining barriers due to awkwardness or possibly guilt that they were doing something that would be so disapproved of in their workplace, and it was at that point that Eddie discovered that passionate sex could also be both demanding and playful. And, oh…*so* satisfying…

It was later, when they slowed down and savoured every moment of doing it all over again, that Eddie realised this was something special.

When he raised his head from the lingering kiss they shared when they'd finally caught their breath again, he had another moment when he imagined he could see past whatever it was that Jodie used so well as a protection for what she didn't want the world to see.

And it almost looked like…a yearning for something?

A wanting of more? More of what they'd just discovered with each other, perhaps?

It was gone so fast it could well have been wishful thinking, replaced by a gleam of what looked a lot more like mischief.

'You're not so bad at that,' Jodie told him.

'I was about to tell you that,' he protested.

They both laughed. But they hadn't broken that eye contact and, when the laughter faded, there it was again. Eddie instinctively let his gaze shift because it felt as if he might be invading Jodie's privacy and he knew she wouldn't like that.

'Are you hungry?' he asked. 'I can offer you some toast. I've even got a jar of Vegemite I brought back from Australia.'

The way Jodie screwed up her nose was the cutest thing Eddie had ever seen. But then she shook her head.

'I should go,' she said.

'You don't have to.'

'Yes, I do.' Jodie was rolling off the side of the bed. Reaching for her tee shirt that was still rolled up into a strange shape. 'Sleeping in my own bed has always been non-negotiable.'

Eddie got out of bed himself and pulled on his jeans as Jodie got dressed. So Jodie had never gone to sleep with someone after having sex? Why not? Had she never felt safe enough with someone to make herself that vulnerable? Or was it the best way to keep something completely casual? To make sex a meaningless hook-up that implied that there was nothing particularly personal involved.

And who was he to judge? Eddie had done that himself on too many occasions in the past. He hadn't had any intention of doing it again, but then he'd never met anyone like Jodie Sinclair, had he? She'd been up for it—as much as he'd ever been and…okay… Mick's accident had been a wakeup call and he wanted something more in his life, but he didn't have to go cold turkey on that new resolution, did he?

One last 'just for fun' encounter had been too tempting to pass up.

Eddie had nothing on but his jeans as he opened the door to let Jodie out into the night. He hadn't even bothered to do up the stud button.

'Want me to walk you to your car?'

'I'm a big girl, Eddie. I can look after myself. And my car's only about two minutes down the road.'

It was the first time she'd called him Eddie, rather than Ed. It made it feel as if something had changed, which was hardly surprising given that they knew each other a hell of a lot better than they had this morning. Her independence was yet another thing he liked about her so he was smiling as he leaned against the door jamb.

'So…' His tone was a question all by itself.

'So what?'

'Do you think it worked?'

'Ah…' Jodie's eyes narrowed a little. 'Did what work, exactly?'

'Did we get it out of our systems?'

He could almost see the lightning-fast progression of her thoughts and the implications of any response she made. In the end, she didn't say anything, but she was trying to hide a smile as she turned away.

''Night, Eddie…'

''Night, Jodie…'

He stood there for a long moment, watching her walk towards her car. She hadn't even given him a hint of an answer to that question, but he realised she hadn't needed to. They both knew the answer, didn't they?

They hadn't got it out of their systems. What they'd done had probably made it even more pervasive. And compelling. But did that matter? If they were both totally on the same page and either of them could call it quits at any time without any hard feelings and simply walk away—the way Jodie was walking away tonight—there was no real reason *not* to do it again.

It was a real shame that Eddie had decided to move on from a casual, friendship with benefits kind of arrangement because he'd never met someone like Jodie who'd been so upfront about not being interested in anything more than sex.

She was, or at least had been, his perfect woman.

* * *

It was a week before Jodie decided she could answer Eddie's question that was, effectively, whether indulging once had been enough as far as getting that sexual attraction to each other out of their systems. She could have answered without hesitation at the time he'd asked, but that had been why she'd waited. To make sure that she was in control.

Of course she was. Okay…maybe she'd been tempted, just for a heartbeat, to stay the rest of the night with Eddie, but she hadn't broken that rule and she wasn't about to. Sleeping with someone was a very different thing to having sex with them. Jodie had always thought it was an even more intimate thing to do. A step closer to a space she wasn't going to ever share again.

She was pleased to discover that she wasn't the only one in control at work as well. Like the aftermath of that kiss that was now ancient history, Eddie didn't give the slightest hint that there was anything happening between them that might be breaking a rule that had become an unwritten law on this rescue base.

It was a busy week that had included a full four-day shift for Blue Watch at Triple A. Four days packed with the usual variety of emergency medical situations. They'd attended several car accidents and a truck that had veered off the road and rolled into a ditch.

They went to a cardiac arrest on a picturesque golf course where the victim was lucky enough to be playing a round with a retired doctor who started CPR and a clubhouse that had an automatic defibrillator that had kick-started a perfusing heart rhythm again despite the blocked cardiac arteries. It had been touch and go to get the man into a catheter laboratory with a second arrest mid-flight but they'd heard later that he'd survived and undergone the bypass surgery he needed.

They'd collected a hiker who'd broken her ankle badly slipping on a track deep within the Cairngorms National Park and there'd been another job the very next day, quite close to that one, where a man who'd been white-water rafting had been thrown into the rapids and hit rocks hard enough to break a few ribs. He'd been in the water for some time before his companions could get him to shore and, by the time the air rescue crew arrived, he was also becoming seriously hypothermic. In an effort to cheer him up, one of his friends had made a joke about nobody wanting to get naked with him to warm him up, like in the movies.

And that joke—or possibly the way Eddie had caught her gaze as they were both smiling—

seemed to have been the catalyst for a definitive decision. The wash of relief Jodie felt when their shift was over for the day and she found Eddie, alone, hanging up his flight suit in the locker room was enough to also make her realise how much she had wanted to give him this answer to that question. Relief mixed with the rather heady thought that, in a very short time, she might be able to feel that delicious anticipation again. A feeling that would probably be all the more intense for both knowing what might lie ahead and having waited this long to experience it again.

'You know those potato skins we left behind at the Pig and Thistle the other night?' she asked.

'Not likely to forget them in a hurry.' Eddie's tone was equally casual. 'Shame we didn't get to finish them.'

'Do you think they might have kept them for us? So we could get them heated up?'

Eddie appeared to give it serious thought. 'I'm sure they thought of doing that, but there are probably some health and safety regulations that prevent them keeping food for a week.'

'Hmm…' This conversational foreplay was more fun than Jodie had expected. 'I suppose we could always buy a fresh basket some time…'

She knew perfectly well that Eddie understood this throwaway suggestion had nothing to do with eating anything at the pub just round the corner from his apartment and she was quite confident that he was about to say he thought it was not a bad idea when the door to the locker room opened and Alex came in.

'So...' Jodie shut the door of her locker with a decisive click as she swallowed her disappointment. 'I'm off to my bouldering session. Fancy a workout, Ed?'

'Is bouldering where you're rock climbing without any safety harnesses or ropes?'

'That's the one.' Jodie grinned at him. 'The risk is minimal when it's inside at the gym and there are nice soft mats on the floor. Alex...do you want to come and give it another go?'

Alex shook his head. 'Once was enough for me, mate. Besides, I'm...busy tonight. Going to a movie.'

'Are you now...?' Eddie gave Alex a direct look. 'It's about time we knew her name, isn't it?'

Alex shrugged. 'Georgia,' he admitted.

'And what does Georgia do?' Jodie also had Alex pinned with her glance.

'She's a nurse at Queen's. In ED.' Alex pulled on his anorak and shut his locker. 'And I'm not answering any more questions. See you guys tomorrow. Have a good night.' He turned as he reached the locker room door. 'You *should* go and try that bouldering,' he told Eddie. 'You might like it a lot more than I did and, even if you don't, you'll discover muscles in the next couple of days that you never knew you had.'

Jodie was looking at Eddie. Alex had just given them the perfect way to be seen spending time together away from work without anyone suspecting that anything else was going on. 'Are you up for it?'

Eddie held her gaze. 'I was born up for it,' he said.

He didn't have to say he was talking about more than a new physical challenge as a work-out. Alex was already out of the door and that message was loud and clear in his eyes.

Jodie smiled. What was even better was that she was still in control and she was going to make this waiting game last a wee bit longer.

'Let's go, then. You can rent some climbing shoes at the gym.'

The relief was almost overwhelming.

It was partly there because Eddie had man-aged to get himself along an albeit beginner's level series of foot and hand holds on the wall of the gymnasium without making a total idiot of himself.

But it was more the relief of discovering that Jodie wanted to spend some time with him again—that she had initiated it herself—when they both knew exactly how it was going to end up. Would it be in her bed this time or back to his place? Not that it mattered. Eddie might be curious to see where she lived but there was plenty of time for that to happen. Plus, he knew that as soon as they touched each other the rest of the world would fade into insignificance, anyway.

It should have been frustrating that they were spending an hour in this noisy gym with a basketball team practice going on in the background and a group of very keen climbers scrambling along this end wall but, in its own way, it was adding to a tension that Eddie hadn't acknowledged had been building for a whole week. Stretching it out a little further was only going to make the breaking of that tension so much better. Possibly better than anything Eddie had ever been lucky enough to experience in his life.

Okay…if being here doing something as acceptable as a gym session after work with a colleague wasn't the best cover they could have come up with for hiding a secret liaison, Eddie might have been tempted to catch Jodie as soon as she finished her higher level scramble and drag her out of the door. Instead, he stood back, shifting to ease muscles all over his body that he suspected he might well be feeling tomorrow and watching Jodie reach for a handhold on an overhang and then stretch her leg to try and find a foothold that would get her higher on the wall. For a moment, she looked like a very, very sexy human starfish.

Eddie blew out a breath, took a glance over his shoulder as if he was also interested in the basketball game going on, although he'd really only wanted to look at the time on a huge wall clock, and then turned back to keep watching Jodie. The climbing session was due to wrap in another five minutes or so.

And he couldn't wait.

He was going to make sure this was an evening that Jodie wouldn't forget in a hurry. One that, hopefully, she wouldn't want to wait a whole week before doing it again.

'Keeping it a secret only makes it better.'

Eddie had been struggling to find a topic of conversation with Mick that might interest him or at least make him smile. He hadn't seen his brother smile once in the last couple of weeks, so when Mick had asked how things were going at work now that he'd had time to settle in properly, he'd found himself confessing what was going on between himself and Jodie Sinclair.

'It started a few weeks ago. You remember I told you about that water rescue training we did on a day off with some of the coastguard volunteers?'

'Yeah…sounded fun.'

'What was even more fun was that Jodie and I ended up at the pub afterwards. We were starving but we ended up not even eating what we'd ordered. Went back to my place instead and… this'll make you laugh… I was in so much of a rush to get her clothes off, I ended up tying her in knots with her own tee shirt.'

'And she came back for more?'

Eddie could feel the warm glow that started something deep in his gut, spreading right to the tips of his fingers and toes.

'Aye…' The affirmative word was almost a sigh and Eddie could feel his face softening with the sound. It was partly due to gratitude that Jodie had not only come back for more but that neither of them seemed at all inclined to put a stop to it yet. Another part of that sound was simply amazement that he could have found someone so like himself. Someone whose company he was so at ease with. They liked the same kind of food. They laughed at the same jokes. They liked pushing themselves to conquer any new challenge, physical or mental. They were passionate about the same work.

'People must have twigged that something's going on between you.' Mick was staring at Eddie. 'Especially if you go around looking like a love-struck puppy, like you're doing right now.'

Eddie adjusted his expression instantly. 'We might like each other,' he admitted. 'But neither of us in "in love". We're friends, that's all.'

Best friends, a small voice at the back of his mind suggested.

Lovers…

If Eddie had ever believed in such a thing as a soul mate, then Jodie would have been at the top of the list of possibilities.

But he didn't believe in the idea of "the one" and, even if he did, Jodie had made it very clear that it wasn't going to be her, so he stifled that unwelcome voice that was coming from nowhere. If the feeling wasn't there on both sides, or if either one or both of the people involved had put up an enormous roadblock so it could never get past a particular point, surely that instantly ruled out the possibility of being someone's perfect partner?

'People know we're friends,' he told Mick. 'And they know we spend time together out of work, but that was Alex's idea.'

'Your crewman?' Mick's jaw dropped. 'He pushed you two together to start dating and you still think nobody knows you're breaking the rules? Or does the secret extend to all your crew members?'

Eddie shook his head. 'Alex suggested Jodie took me to her bouldering class because he didn't want to go back to it. They think I fell in love with the sport and they think it's a great idea. The base operations manager even suggested we both got into some abseiling as well because they're the sort of skills that could come in handy on a mission when we can't get anyone from a mountain rescue team on scene quickly. Jodie's keen because that would mean she could free climb up wild cliffs and then abseil down and save time before having another go.' He grinned at Mick. 'So there you go—we have one night every week when we're expected to spend time together. Plus, it's an excuse to get out on our days off—to go hiking and look for some wild rocks to play around on.'

'Play around on is right,' Mick muttered. 'And I don't believe you're going to be able to keep it secret.'

'We're managing so far.'

They were so good at switching off any personal connection at work, in fact, that as far as Gus and Alex were concerned, Eddie and Jodie had just welded themselves into a tight, professional team. The connection between them actually improved their professional relationship—as though there was an element of communication where they could read each other's body language so well, it was almost like telepathy.

'You'd better make the most of it while it lasts.' Mick's tone was a warning.

'I intend to.' Eddie nodded. 'Who wouldn't? Jimmy wasn't wrong—there *are* some girls who just want to play. And man… I've never found a playtime like this before. It's perfect.'

'Lucky you.' Mick shook his head. 'But I hope you're being careful about more than just keeping it a secret. What are you going to do if she gets pregnant?'

'She won't.' Eddie was more than confident on that score. 'She's passionate about her career and she's got no interest in a long-term relationship—with anyone. Having a kid would be the last thing she'd want. Besides, you taught me well. I'm always careful.'

'Should have listened to my own advice, shouldn't I?' There was a smile on Mick's face now but it was too wry to count as something positive. 'And been a bit more careful myself.'

Eddie's heart broke a little more. He hated that his brother was having to go through this and now he felt guilty that he'd been telling him how amazing his sex life currently was. But it wouldn't feel right to be hiding what was going on in his own life from his brother and maybe continuing to treat Mick with kid gloves, saying only supportive things and letting Mick take this journey at his own pace wasn't going to help in the long run.

Mick was cooperating with everything being asked of him in the way of occupational and physiotherapy and his upper body strength was improving to the point where he could wheel his chair. He was close to being able to transfer himself from bed to chair as well, which would be a big step towards independence, but it felt like Mick saw it more as an admission of failure that he would never walk again. He had regained almost normal sensation in his legs some time ago but the hope of that becoming meaningful movement was beginning to fade and nobody would be surprised if Mick had actually lost hope.

Letting him bemoan things that had happened in the past certainly wasn't going to help anything either, but assuming that when Mick had said he should have been more careful he'd been referring to being jilted on his wedding day after believing he was about to become a father was an easier route to take for Eddie. It suddenly felt too daunting to open the can of worms that was how Mick was feeling about his future.

'Oh, come on...' Eddie made his tone amused. 'You were over Juliana by the end of that pity party we all had on your non-wedding day. If I remember correctly, it was you who declared that we would only ever need each other?'

Mick looked away. 'Sorry,' he muttered. 'I know I'm being a wet blanket. I'm glad you're having fun with Jodie.'

'Just trying to emulate your exploits.' Eddie grinned. 'I lost count of how many women there were after Juliana. It was like you were single-handedly trying to prove that you were the over-all winner of the "Fearsome Threesome" that Ella used to call us.'

'My ears are burning…' Ella walked into Mick's room as Eddie was speaking. She had the strap of a laptop bag over her shoulder and looked like a woman on a mission. 'Are you talk-ing about me?'

'Not exactly.'

'Did you both get Jimmy's text?'

'My phone battery's dead,' Mick said. 'But Eddie told me it's about the locum position in Aberdeen. He's coming up next month?'

'He is.'

'Does the position come with accommoda-tion? Like you had when you came here?'

'Possibly.' Ella nodded. 'But we've suggested he stays at our place. House-sitting.'

'House-sitting? Where are you and Logan going? You *never* take holidays.'

'Exactly.' Ella perched on the end of the bed. 'We've never even had a honeymoon so we de-cided that this was an opportunity we couldn't pass up. Jimmy's going to house-sit for us and we're going on honeymoon. To New Zealand.'

'New Zealand?' The surprise had been enough to catch Mick's interest. 'Wow…now there's a place that I've always fancied visiting. I should have done when you were in Australia, Eddie. Missed my chance, didn't I?'

'Funny you should say that…' Ella was unpacking her laptop. 'Because when Logan and I were searching destinations we came across something that I thought might interest you.' She clicked on a link and then put the computer on Mick's lap. 'Don't say anything,' she told him. 'Just have a look. I'll send you the link so you can look at it more thoroughly later, if you've got your own laptop charged.'

'What is it?' Eddie got to his feet to peer over his brother's shoulder. He could see slide show images changing automatically. Gorgeous scenery of mountains and beaches and forests. Happy, smiling people. What looked like a state-of-the-art gymnasium. And…wheelchairs? Yes…there were people wearing what looked like designer uniforms. Including a very gorgeous young woman with long blonde hair and a smile with a wattage that would be enough to power a small town.

'It's a rather exclusive rehab centre.' It sounded like Ella was making an effort to keep her tone casual. 'On the Coromandel Peninsula, which is not far from Auckland in New Zealand and looks like one of the most beautiful parts of an already gorgeous country.'

'I've been there,' Eddie said. 'Just for a couple of days but it was incredible. I'd go back in a heartbeat.'

'Sorry, we're not inviting you.' But Ella was smiling. 'We thought that Mick deserved a bit of a break if he felt like it. We'd like *you* to come with us.'

'To *New Zealand*? To play gooseberry on your *honeymoon*?' Mick gave a huff of laughter. 'You have got to be kidding.'

'Nope.' Ella waved her hand, dismissing his reaction. 'We're not suggesting you come everywhere with us, but we'd travel with you and stay while you got settled in for your own holiday. And then we'll get a camper van and drive all the way down to the South Island and back again. We thought if we were going to go that far, we might as well do it properly. We've both got a ton of leave to use up and cover's been arranged so we're thinking at least a month. You could come back with us, Mick or…if you like the place you could stay for longer. It'll be summer there and it might be good to escape the worst of a Scottish winter. They also have an amazing reputation for what they can do for spinal injury patients. Anyway...'

Ella didn't elaborate on the comment. 'I can't stay,' she told Mick. 'I'm on call for the obstetric emergency response team tonight so I need to get back. I just popped in to tell you about this.'

'You could have just emailed the link.'

'You might have just deleted it.' There was something in Ella's tone that made Eddie think she might also be thinking that some kind of change was needed in the way they were supporting Mick. Letting him just slide further into shutting himself off from the world wasn't an acceptable option.

Mick picked up the laptop to hand back to her and he must have touched the mousepad that stopped the slide show continuing to loop. The image on the screen was that of the blonde woman in her designer scrub suit with the dancing blue eyes and that smile that suggested life couldn't get any better.

Eddie could see Mick staring at it, his eyes narrowed as if the screen—or that smile—was bright enough to be hurting his eyes. He caught Ella's gaze as she took the laptop back and knew that the tiny shake of his head, unseen by Mick, was enough to convey his opinion that this was a great idea but there was very little chance that Mick was going to agree to visit a new rehab centre, no matter how beautiful the setting was. Or any of the therapists on the staff, for that matter.

It was a fantasy rehab centre.

Too good to be true?

Eddie felt a trickle of sensation run down his spine that felt almost like a premonition. Was what he and Jodie had found with each other too good to be true?

Was it going to crash and burn?

No...

'I need to head off too,' he told Mick. 'I've got a bouldering session at the gym this evening and I'm going to finally get myself off the beginner's level.'

'Don't break anything,' Mick warned. 'I'm the only one in the family who's allowed to be out of action.' He winked at Eddie. 'Get out there and wave the flag for the "Fearsome Threesome".'

'Will do my best.' Eddie gave his brother a fist bump after Mick had tried, and failed, to escape his sister's kiss.

He followed Ella from the room, confident that he wasn't going to break anything in the near future—including the fantasy relationship he was lucky enough to be enjoying with Jodie Sinclair.

CHAPTER SEVEN

ABERDEEN AIR AMBULANCE'S annual fundraiser was an event that was circled on a huge number of local calendars judging by the crowds that gathered every year, especially when the weather was as kind as it was today, which was a huge relief. Like the vast majority of air ambulance helicopters in the UK, Triple A had to be funded by a charity organisation and there was an army of faithful volunteers—often including the patients and families of people whose lives had been saved by the service—who put in a massive amount of work to make this event as successful as possible.

The star of the show—the gleaming black H145 helicopter that Gus and Alex had polished to perfection this morning—was hovering above that crowd, giving them time to finish the important things they were doing, like getting their faces painted, being given the paper cone of hot chips they'd ordered, climbing out of the bouncy castle or just going to the loo. Everybody wanted to get to a good spot around the edges of the football field to see the drama of the close-up winching demonstration that was about to happen, that would give them a taste of what the air ambulance might do when it received an emergency call.

The Blue Watch crew were more than happy to sit well above the scene for a while and let the anticipation build. There was quite enough to be looking at to keep them entertained.

'This is a much bigger deal than I expected it to be,' Eddie said. 'It looks like a cross between a funfair and some Highland games. Is that a pipe band on that stage?'

'Aye.' Alex was grinning. 'And when you and Jodie are talking to all the wee bairns who want to come and have a look at the helicopter, me and Gus are going to have a go at tossing a caber.'

Jodie laughed. 'No, you won't. You both have to stay with the chopper and help entertain the masses.'

'I'm not going anywhere,' Gus muttered. 'I'll be too busy keeping all those sticky fingers off my paintwork.'

'You'd be lucky to be able to pick one of those logs up with you both holding each end of it,' Jodie said. 'You do realise they can weigh nearly as much as you do, Alex, don't you?'

'I'll use one of the little ones they've got for

the kids to try out.' But Alex turned to look at Jodie. 'How do you know how much I weigh, anyway?'

'You know it's one of my splinter skills.' Jodie's smile was smug. 'I like to estimate how much a patient weighs so that I know when to save my back from getting wrecked by calling in lifting assistance from someone else on scene. Like a firie or two.'

'Speaking of firies...' Eddie craned his head to see beneath them. 'I can see a couple of ambulances, which is fair enough given the first aid cover you'd need for an event of this size, but what's the fire engine down there for?'

'We get support from all the emergency services,' Jodie said. 'There'll be a police car somewhere as well, but the fire truck is a favourite for the kiddies. They can buy a ticket and get a ride on it.'

'No pony rides, then?'

'They might get a bit freaked out when we get low enough to do our demo,' Gus put in. 'Don't think anyone wants to cope with ponies bolting through a crowd like that. How's it looking down there? Is our audience in place?'

Eddie eyed the rows of people forming behind the ropes that were keeping them well away from the centre of the football field. 'Looks like half the crowd is there. I'm thinking the rest will be able to see most of it from where they are.'

'Aye…' Alex attached his strop to the safety anchor. 'I wouldn't be giving up my spot in the kebab queue just to watch you and Jodie dangling in mid-air.'

'That's because you get to see it all the time.' Jodie wagged her finger at him. 'You're spoilt, you are.'

Eddie didn't seem to be sharing the joke. 'I hope that bouncy castle's well tied down,' he said.

'I'm sure it is,' Jodie said. 'But that's a good point. Gus, can you radio through to the event management team and get them to make sure nobody's inside the castle—or those big ball things—when we're landing?'

'Roger that.'

Jodie turned her head in time to catch an intensity in Eddie's eyes that made her heart skip a beat.

'You weren't there, were you?' she asked. 'At that terrible accident in Tasmania a few years ago?'

'No. But I had a very good friend who was in one of the first helicopters to arrive on scene. She had such bad PTSD afterwards, she ended up walking away from her career. Last I heard, she had no intention of going back.'

She...

A very good friend. Someone he was still in contact with?

The flash of something like jealousy took Jodie completely off-guard and it was strong enough to be...ridiculous...that was what it was. As if she and Eddie were in a deeply significant relationship and she'd just found out he was cheating on her?

Or perhaps it was something else that was messing with her head. That hint of pain in Eddie's voice? That knot in her gut that was an empathy with how profoundly he cared about other people? Both the female paramedic he knew and the children who had been involved in an accident that had hit headlines around the world.

'It was a really freak gust of wind, wasn't it? I read that it might have been a mini tornado.'

'I heard about it too.' Alex nodded. 'The castle got lifted about thirty feet into the air. What was it—five kids that died?'

'Six in the end,' Eddie said quietly. 'One died later in hospital.'

Gus spoke calmly. 'It's all good here,' he said. 'They've already closed the area with the bouncy castle and the human hamster balls. They won't open them until we've landed and shut down and then they'll close them again when we're due to take off.'

'That's hours away,' Alex informed them. 'Isn't it grand that we get to spend our whole day off together?'

'Yeah, right...'

Jodie laughed, happy to see that Eddie was smiling again. As her gaze brushed his, she knew he wasn't complaining about the company. It was easy to see that he wanted to be with her and time outside of a shift when their patients were their first priority was a real bonus. Not quite on the same level as when they had their secret, private times together but it was still a bonus.

For both of them.

'It's two minutes to show time.' Gus sounded focused on what they were really here for—to showcase the equipment and skills they had available to save lives and encourage people to spend their money and buy raffle tickets and rides and make donations that would help the organisation keep running and provide an even better service over the coming year.

'I'll do a circuit around the whole field and then get a bit lower,' he added. 'We'll do the winch demonstration and then land dead centre. You guys all ready?'

The winch demonstration was a rerun of what they'd done on their sea rescue training day. Gus kept the helicopter steady at a low enough level to give their audience the thrill of feeling the wash and not only hearing the beat of the rotors. Jodie got winched down to the grassy field and unhooked herself and then Eddie went down, put her in a nappy harness and Alex winched them both back up to the helicopter.

Jodie knew that someone would be giving an explanation over the loudspeakers to the crowd about what was happening so she hoped they would be able to hear it over the noise of the hovering helicopter. At least Alex knew how to play to the crowd and he made it a slow ascent. So slow that it felt like they were simply hanging in the air without moving at all at one point.

Not that Jodie minded. The harness wasn't the most comfortable thing to be wearing once it was carrying her weight but she didn't mind at all that her hips were between Eddie's legs and the point of contact for her body was against his lower abdomen.

Quite the opposite.

She was loving it. She enjoyed Eddie's company as much as he seemed to enjoy hers. He was an intelligent and funny companion and they had so much in common that they never ran out of things to talk about. Jodie might not have met any of Eddie's family members, of course, with them keeping their private time together such a secret, but she felt as if she knew them now.

She knew how close to his brothers Eddie was and how much he was worried about Mick. She knew that he adored his big half-sister, Ella, who was eight years older than the triplets and had been another mother to them when their shared mother's IVF treatment had been unexpectedly too successful and had instantly doubled the size of their family. She knew how hard it had been on Eddie and his brothers when his mother had lost her battle to cancer when they were only teenagers and that their broken-hearted father had died not long after.

Eddie said that was why the siblings had all ended up with medical careers but Jodie knew there was more to it than personal tragedy, at least in Eddie's case. He had always been destined to do a job that was focused on people because he was a person who genuinely cared about others.

A kind man.

She liked him. A lot. This day together really was a bonus and she intended to enjoy every minute of it. And when it was finished, she knew that Eddie would probably be as keen as she was to spend some more time together because it had been nearly a week since they'd been together in the way that was starting to haunt her nights when she was at home by herself.

Together alone.

In Eddie's apartment.

In Eddie's bed…

And Jodie loved the anticipation of that too. She was loving almost everything about Eddie, to be honest. She loved how casual things were. How astonishingly good the sex was. How surprisingly easy it seemed to be to keep it a secret.

It had been going on a lot longer than she'd expected it to, mind you, but why fix something if it wasn't broken? Jodie had never found someone who seemed to feel exactly the same way she did about long-term relationships or anything that might require commitment of some kind. She liked him enough for a friendship to be more than welcome and, hopefully, that could continue when they'd finally had enough sex to be able to agree that the unusually distracting level of attraction to each other had worn off.

Which would be soon, she was sure of it.

Just…not *quite* yet.

Safely back in the cabin of the helicopter, they kept the door open and waved at the crowd as Gus brought the aircraft down to land on the grass. Event officials were preparing to shift ropes and do some crowd control to let people closer to talk to the crew, look inside the helicopter and ask what Jodie knew from experience would be endless questions from both children and adults as the crew watched to make sure that everyone and everything stayed where they were supposed to be and remained undamaged.

It would be full-on and could be seen as a chore, given that it was sucking up one of Blue Watch's days off, but it always felt like a privilege to be involved in a public relations exercise like this. To be a face of a service that she was so proud to be a part of.

On top of that, probably for the rest of Jodie's life, doing something extra like this, especially if it involved a winching demonstration, was always going to remind her of when it had all started with Eddie, wasn't it? When being in such close physical contact as he'd winched her up from the sea had made that attraction between them spiral so completely out of control. It seemed ages ago now but, because their 'arrangement' was so casual and it was disguised so well by their apparently mutual interest in bouldering, it was nothing to worry about so there hadn't been any need to pull the plug on it just yet.

It wasn't as if they had even spent a whole night together because Jodie made sure they only went to Eddie's apartment so that she was always in control and could leave whenever she chose, but what would happen when they went away for a weekend together? When they could be sharing a motel unit, for example? Would she break her ironclad rule of not falling asleep in the same bed—let alone the arms—of a sexual partner?

There was just such a weekend coming up soon, with an abseiling course high in the Cairngorms and, ironically, it had been Dion who'd heard about it and persuaded both Eddie and Jodie to enrol. An all-expenses-paid weekend away to enhance skills that would be valuable within the team of rescue medics. It would be a great cover, if they needed one, to spend some time together this evening. If anyone noticed, it would be a perfectly reasonable excuse to want to discuss the upcoming course and go through the list of gear they needed to take. As a local, Jodie could tell Eddie where to go shopping for any outdoor clothing or other essentials he might not have. She might even go with him if they had time before the shopping centres closed.

Given the length of time that Jodie had been working with Eddie now, it shouldn't have come as a surprise that he was so good at interacting with people in this kind of social situation. After all, he could charm little old ladies and reassure frightened people with an ease she'd seen him employ with everybody he came into contact with through his work.

Like he had on his first day at work with Triple A, when he'd crouched beside that young mountain biker, Caitlin, and smiled at her.

Sorry we took so long, sweetheart...

Jodie could still hear that tone in his voice. The one that had almost made her envious of their patient. Now she was enjoying hearing snatches of his voice, when she wasn't talking herself, as they both got on with talking to the eager crowds of children and teenagers pushing in to get a closer look at the helicopter and ask their pressing questions. Some event officials were helping to protect the aircraft and their gear because Gus and Alex had been sent off to wander through the crowd to chat to people and help sell raffle tickets. When they came back, the biggest raffle prizes would be drawn in front of the helicopter and then it would be time for them to take off and head back to base.

Currently, Jodie was sitting at the helicopter's rear cabin opening—between the open clam-shell doors beneath the tail—to keep an eye on their stretcher, which they'd put on the grass to act as a display shelf for some of their equipment. She only had to turn her head to see Eddie sitting in the other open door—the one they would slide open to winch out of.

A proud mother was urging a small boy, with a mop of red curls, who looked about five years old to step forward to talk to Eddie. He'd already been to a face-painting station and he had the blue and white Scottish flag on one cheek and the Triple A logo on the other. He was also clutching a soft toy replica of one of the air rescue's black helicopters.

'Do you like working on the helicopter?' he asked Eddie shyly.

Eddie, sitting in the open cabin doorway, smiled at the boy. 'What's your name, buddy?'

'Connor.'

'Are you old enough to keep a secret, Connor?'

Connor nodded solemnly. 'I'm *five*,' he told Eddie.

'Okay... Don't tell anybody but...' Eddie leaned closer and spoke in a stage whisper that even Jodie could hear. 'It's the very best job in the whole wide world.'

Connor's eyes were huge.

'What do you want to do when you grow up?' Eddie asked.

Connor took a visibly deep breath, stood on tiptoes and whispered something in Eddie's ear that made him grin widely.

'I'll keep the seat warm for you, buddy,' he said.

Something was melting deep within Jodie's chest as she watched the exchange. Maybe it was the hero worship in those big eyes under the shaggy red curls of the child's hair. Or the way Eddie had bent his head so that the secret that was being whispered was something special that was just between the two of them.

Whatever it was, it touched something that felt surprisingly tender. It made Jodie think of how Eddie would be with his own children one day in the future.

And that shouldn't have bothered her because Jodie had made peace long ago with the idea that there weren't going to be children in her own future—either in partnership with their father or as a single mother. She'd smacked the button on her biological clock to silence any alarm and, okay…she was going to miss out on things that other people considered the most important part of their lives, but there were plenty of other people who were happy and fulfilled without having children of their own and she was one of them.

Something else she'd learned about Eddie's family, in fact, was that his sister felt the same way. After spending so many years mothering her much younger brothers, she'd always said she didn't want to have any children of her own. She'd 'been there, done that' according to Eddie and she didn't need to do it again. If things were different, Jodie would have liked to meet Eddie's sister. To get to know his whole family, even.

But things weren't different and Jodie was still

damping down the hotspots of an unexpected emotional reaction to the thought of Eddie having a child of his own—with some unknown woman he was going to meet in the future—when she turned her head to see a teenager who was reaching to push a button on the defibrillator that was attached to a frame that would have gone over a patient's feet if someone had been lying on the stretcher.

'Don't touch that.' Jodie's warning came out more sharply than she had intended. 'That's an expensive bit of kit and we can't afford to have it damaged.'

'I just wanted to see how it worked.'

'Well…' Jodie sucked in a breath. She could see little red-haired Connor walking away with his mother and knew that Eddie was glancing in her direction, perhaps because he'd heard her snap at someone? 'I can tell you anything you want to know.'

'Why's it got so many buttons?'

'Because it can do so many cool things. It can take your blood pressure, tell us how much oxygen you've got in your blood, whether your heart is beating normally and it can give you an electric shock to help restart your heart if it's stopped.'

'Like on telly when you hold those things

on top of them and yell at everyone to "Stand Clear"?'

'We don't use paddles any more. We have sticky patches and electrodes that clip onto them. They're much safer.'

The teenager shrugged. 'Not so cool, though.'

'The people that need their hearts started again don't seem to mind. And we do still have to tell people to stand clear.'

'Can it take my blood pressure?'

'I don't see why not.' Jodie found a smile. 'Take your anorak off and then sit down on the stretcher here.' She patted the end. 'Roll up the sleeve of your jumper too. I'll need one of your arms above the elbow.'

She opened a pouch on the side of the defibrillator case and took out the blood pressure cuff, turned the machine on and plugged the cord attached to the cuff into its slot. A small crowd was gathering as she wrapped the cuff around the teenager's arm.

'This will start getting tighter on your arm as soon as I push the button,' she warned. 'It has to get tight enough to stop the blood getting into your arm, but it's only for a second and then you'll feel it getting loose again. Keep still and you'll see the numbers coming up on the screen. You can see your heart rate already, see? It's only sixty, which tells me you're probably quite fit. Do you play sports?'

'Bit of footie.' But the lad puffed out his chest a bit. 'And I ride my bike.'

'Keep it up. It's good being fit.' Jodie reached into the pouch again for the finger clip. 'Here… we'll put a pulse oximeter on your finger too and see what percentage of oxygen you've got in your blood.'

The teenager grinned at his mates who were watching, delighted to be the centre of attention. As his facial expression exaggerated how uncomfortably tight the cuff was becoming, Jodie noticed that Eddie had joined the spectators and he was enjoying her 'patient's' reaction. He'd be just as good at handling his teenaged son as making them feel special when they were five years old, she thought.

But he had a woman beside him who had a baby in a front pack and Jodie couldn't help imagining Eddie wearing a pack like that or with a baby in his arms and that tender spot in her chest was being touched again. This time, hard enough to hurt. It wasn't simply imagining that faceless woman in his future who would be the mother of his children. It was all too easy to imagine how it would feel to trust this man enough to start thinking about building a future with him.

Building a family.

Having his baby...

But what was a whole lot worse than imagining it as an abstract concept involving that faceless partner, Jodie was doing more than tapping into feeling a part of that picture.

She *wanted* to be a part of it.

It was only the tiniest, embryonic seed of a feeling but it was a yearning that she knew had the capacity to be so potent—and dangerous—that Jodie found herself unable to release the breath she had in her lungs. Dear Lord...she'd never been this close to losing control of her emotions in private, let alone in a public arena. She could almost feel tears prickling at the back of her eyes. Just blinking hard, once, was enough to send them packing, mind you. And focusing on what she was doing dealt with any other wayward thoughts.

'There you go. Your blood pressure is one hundred and ten over seventy, which is perfectly normal for your age group. Your oxygen saturation is a hundred percent too. You get top marks.' The sound of Velcro ripping apart punctuated her sentence as she removed the blood pressure cuff. 'Anyone else want their blood pressure taken?'

The chorus of assent was so enthusiastic Jodie knew she'd be kept very busy for the rest of her time at this event. And that was fine. Exactly what she needed. She might even add to the busyness and offer to do a demonstration of a three-lead ECG or find someone who was brave enough to have a finger prick so that she could test their blood glucose level. This was what they were here for, after all—to make the public aware of what they could do and help support the service with the kind of extra funding that could provide the latest model of a piece of equipment like this defibrillator.

Eddie was just as busy. He was showing someone how to step into a nappy harness that could be used to winch them up from an accident scene if they weren't so badly injured they needed a stretcher. Jodie looked past him to see if she could spot Gus or Alex coming back their way. A bit of extra help would be great, but what would be even better would be to get this gig done and dusted so that she could get home and go for a long, long run.

And do a bit of boxing as well.

Whatever it took to get this new tension out of her body and her head back into a space that she felt comfortable with, because otherwise it had the potential to morph into a sense of panic and Jodie Sinclair would not permit that to happen. The first step of making that process effective was, fortunately, already crystal-clear. She had become too close to Edward Grisham and she had to dial it back before it got any worse.

Way back.

She'd known that the aspects of their relationship that crossed the acceptable boundaries of friendship would have to stop soon, but had it really only been on the way here to this event that she'd been thinking that it didn't have to end quite yet?

How wrong had she been?

It had already gone on far too long. She'd slipped into a forbidden comfort zone and hadn't even noticed that safety barriers were being lowered. Seriously damaged, even? She'd been seduced by the feeling of being able to trust as much as she had by any irresistible physical pull towards Eddie.

She should have ended their illicit liaison long ago.

No. She should never have let it start, but she had. Willingly. Now she had to deal with getting out of it.

Back to safety.

CHAPTER EIGHT

HE HADN'T SEEN it coming.

Well…that wasn't exactly true, was it? Eddie had known right from the start that what was going on between himself and Jodie was never going to be long-term. He just hadn't expected to be blindsided by how suddenly it had been terminated. He certainly hadn't anticipated it being the footnote of what had otherwise been a very enjoyable day of taking part in the annual fundraiser for the air rescue base.

As soon as they'd lifted clear of the football field, in fact, with a cheering crowd waving them off. It was only a few minutes flying time before they'd get back to base, but it was enough time for Jodie to not only drop her bombshell but to make it seem like no more than a casual dismissal.

Eddie had been the one to suggest a drink and perhaps a pub dinner later that evening at the Pig and Thistle.

'It's Saturday night, after all, and I don't know

about you guys, but I was a bit disappointed I didn't get the chance to get a kebab or some hot chips from one of those food stalls.'

'I've got plans later but I'd be up for a quick beer first,' Gus said.

'I'm in.' Alex nodded. 'Georgia's on night shift.'

'Count me out this time.' Jodie's tone was oddly offhand, which Eddie instinctively knew was significant. 'I've got other plans tonight.'

She hadn't even glanced in Eddie's direction but then he was trying not to stare at her. Or to react to what felt like a bit of a slap, to be honest.

But perhaps he was overreacting? Eddie waited a beat but knew he had an easy way to find out. He kept his tone just as casual as Jodie's had been.

'Do you want to pop into that adventure clothing outlet on your way home? I could meet you there.' Gus was already bringing the helicopter down on his approach to land on the platform outside the hangar. 'Doesn't shut for another half an hour and I need some good waterproof gear for that abseiling trip. What was it you wanted? New gloves?'

'There's plenty of time for me to do that next week.' Jodie's smile was perfectly friendly. As teasing as her tone, even. 'You don't need me to hold your hand while you go shopping, Eddie.

As long as you don't buy some fluorescent pink over-pants, of course.'

Her gaze only grazed his but it was enough to send the silent message that time together out of work hours was definitely not on Jodie's agenda today. Maybe not tomorrow either. Had she, for no discernible reason, even decided that she no longer wanted it at all?

And…dammit…

It *hurt*…

Maybe he'd known it could never last, but why hadn't she just talked to him about it when they were alone? They could have agreed to stay friends. He would have respected her decision.

Or would he? Maybe Jodie was giving him this message in front of their colleagues as a reminder that they'd been lucky not to get caught out before this. Maybe she knew that if they were alone he would have tried to persuade her that it could continue for just a little longer.

One more night…?

And why not? Maybe what was really bothering Eddie was that he didn't really understand why it was happening like this. It wasn't as if anyone else knew what was going on. Or that he'd given any indication that he wanted something more than Jodie was prepared to give which, in the past, had always been when an alarm had rung loudly enough to prompt Eddie to find the kindest but quickest way to stop things going any further.

Okay…maybe this was karma. He'd done this to so many women he had no right to feel that it was unjustified to have the shoe on the other foot. Jodie had always had the right to back off from the intimate extension to their professional relationship whenever she chose to and he had to respect that, even if it might be the last thing *he* wanted.

Gus was shutting down the engines and the rotors were already slowing. The snap of safety belts being unfastened sounded like a punctuation mark to more than the short flight home.

Eddie reached to slide open the door.

'No worries,' he said. 'But I'm not making any promises about the pink pants.'

Alex was laughing. 'It's not a bad idea, actually. Nice and easy to spot when someone has to come and rescue you out in the wilderness of the Cairngorms.'

With another crew on duty today, there was no reason to leave this helicopter outside and there were chores to do to make sure any equipment that had been on display or used during its time at the fundraising event was clean, tidy or replaced, ready for when it would be used for its normal workload again—which could be any time at all, if a big emergency occurred and every resource the city had needed to be deployed.

Eddie had assumed Jodie would take care of the defibrillator that she'd been using this afternoon. After the popularity of people having a three-lead ECG taken, it was highly likely that the pouch containing the electrodes needed topping up and the batteries would need to be changed for fully charged ones. But Jodie simply got out and walked away and Eddie felt himself frowning.

Something wasn't right.

He unclipped the defibrillator from its shelf. 'Back in a minute,' he told Alex.

'Hey…' He caught up with Jodie before she entered the hangar.

Was it his imagination or did Jodie flinch just a little when she heard his voice?

No… When she automatically flicked her gaze upwards at the same time, Eddie caught a glimpse of something in her eyes that he'd never seen before.

Fear…?

His mouth suddenly felt dry. 'What's up?' he asked quietly. 'Jodie, are you okay?'

Whatever it was he thought he'd seen—or perhaps felt—in her expression had vanished and Eddie felt the tension that was making it hard to breathe start to release its grip on his chest.

Maybe whatever was going on had nothing to do with him? With *them*?

'I'm fine.'

Sometimes silence could be more significant than any words that could be found and, sure enough, Jodie filled the gap by the time they were in the middle of the hangar, halfway between the storeroom and the locker room.

'Okay… It's just… I realised that it's become a bit of a habit, Eddie. And the longer habits are there, the harder they can be to break and…if that happens, breaking them is bound to cause a bit of collateral damage.'

He didn't have to ask what she meant. She was talking about them. About the sex. The best sex he'd ever had the privilege of discovering. He wasn't sure whether Jodie was thinking that it becoming a habit would mean they became complacent and their secret would be found out or that she considered the collateral damage would include emotional pain for either of them but, if things got messy, they both knew it could mean they'd never work together again. And if someone had to leave the base completely, it would definitely be Eddie because he'd only been here such a short time.

Eddie didn't want that to happen.

Did that explain what he thought he'd read in her eyes? Or had she been afraid of telling him?

Was she worried that he might be hurt? That *she* might be hurt if they took this any further?

Eddie didn't want that to happen either. Even the possibility of Jodie being hurt outweighed any emotional discomfort he might need to deal with himself.

'It's okay, Jodie,' he said. 'It's your call. We both knew it had a "use-by" date.'

Jodie nodded but her gaze dropped. 'I should do the defib,' she said. 'I was the one playing with it all afternoon.'

'I've got this.' Eddie found a smile. 'We're a team, remember?' He waited to catch her gaze lifting so that she would know he was trying to reassure her that he was going to do his best to make the transition from friends with benefits to simply friends as painless as possible. '*We've* got this,' he added quietly. 'And, hey...'

'What?'

'I promise I won't buy any pink pants.'

Jodie was laughing as she turned away to head for the locker room and Eddie's smile was genuine now. He might have just lost something that had become important in his life but he was damned if he was going to let their very real friendship vanish as well.

He'd meant that promise. He was going to make this change in their personal connection easy. Hopefully, they could still work together without any issues. Have social time with the whole crew together. Perhaps they would both even be able to cherish memories of how good it had—briefly—been between them.

The Saturday following the fundraising event was the last working day for Blue Watch's next roster and Jodie was finally starting to feel as if she could relax.

She wasn't needing to keep herself busy between callouts with less than urgent tidying or stocktaking in the storeroom or cleaning and sorting gear that hadn't been used in recent times. She could be in the staffroom, sitting at the table having a coffee with the rest of her crew and other staff members around.

Including Eddie.

In a way, nothing had changed because—as far as she could tell—nobody else had had any idea what had been going on between herself and Eddie. They'd successfully kept both their attraction to each other and what they'd ended up doing to get it 'out of their systems' a secret.

But too much had changed for Jodie because she was still so aware of his presence. She could still feel that pull towards him that had become such a pleasant frisson of both the emotional and physical history they'd created with each other and the anticipation of building on it even more.

Now there was only the history and Jodie was missing that anticipation.

She was missing being alone with Eddie, but that was only strengthening her resolve to stay well away from him. That odd feeling of panic she'd experienced at the fundraising event had subsided, thank goodness, but it had given her a painful wake-up call. She wasn't as bullet-proof as she'd thought she was, was she?

Since then, however, during the rest of her days off and with even more determination, when she was back at work, Jodie had reminded herself that her career was the only thing she was truly passionate about in her life. She didn't want a meaningful relationship, let alone children—with Eddie or anyone else—and that tiny seed of yearning that had sprouted in such an unwelcome fashion had been firmly rooted out. She'd kept her guard up constantly at work, just to be on the safe side, but now she was realising she didn't need to.

Eddie was keeping that promise he'd made and he was making this easy. Nothing had changed with their ability to work together so well.

He didn't seem upset at all that their fling was over either. He still seemed to be enjoying her company. Wanting to keep their friendship intact.

Jodie wanted that as well. And as soon as

she'd filed those memories into a compartment that she could choose whether or not to open, normal life would resume and everything would be good again.

Better than good. She'd never had a colleague that she could trust to the extent she trusted Eddie and that made a huge difference when a call came in that they just knew was going to be a big one.

Just such a call came through late on that Saturday afternoon.

'Car versus truck.' Dion came into the staffroom as their pagers were sounding. 'Multiple casualties. There's an ambulance crew on scene and they've done an initial triage and say they've got one Status Zero and one, possibly two, Status Ones and a Status Two. They can't be sure because they need the fire service to get access to the car.'

Everyone was on their feet already and heading for the door and stairs down to the hangar. A Status Zero meant that there'd been a fatality and Status Ones were serious enough to be in danger of losing their lives without immediate medical intervention. A Status Two patient also needed urgent medical care.

'All available road crews are being diverted,' Dion called after them. 'And a fire crew has just located on scene. If there are any other helicopters available they'll be on standby and I'll alert our backup crew.'

Blue Watch lifted up from the helipad within the next two minutes. The cockpit screens were updating with all the details they needed, including the exact location of the accident, which was on the outskirts of Aberdeen, on a road with a rural speed limit high enough to mean that a collision would be serious. The truck had come in from a side road.

'There's a quarry up there,' Alex said grimly. 'If that truck was carrying a load of rock, it would be heavy enough to have hit anything else on the road like a bomb going off.'

'There's multiple nose-to-tail impacts behind the car too.' Jodie was reading the screen on her tablet. 'There's something that doesn't quite add up here. Why were there so many vehicles on that section of a country road?'

'Maybe the first car was going slowly enough to hold them up,' Eddie suggested. 'That can cause a bit of road rage and it only takes one stupid move to set off a chain reaction that can be catastrophic.'

Gus was on a radio channel with emergency service personnel on the ground. 'They've closed the road to traffic in both directions to give us a landing area on the tarmac,' he reported. 'But we've got power lines on one side and some trees on the other. Second option is a field, but they'll need to cut access through a hedgerow and a fence and there may be some sheep in there. We'll do a circuit and check it out.'

They could all see the line of stalled traffic snaking along a road bordering a tributary of the River Dee. The flashing lights of the emergency services already on scene were visible next and a low, slow circuit gave Gus and the crew the chance to choose their best landing spot.

'It's a limousine,' Eddie pointed out. 'With a side impact from that truck that's rolled.'

Jodie's heart sank. The occupants of a luxury limousine were unlikely to have been wearing safety belts.

'That might explain the convoy of traffic behind them,' Alex said. 'It could be a wedding party. There's an old castle further along the river that's a popular venue for receptions.'

'We'll land on the road,' Gus decided. 'The sooner we get you guys down there, the better.'

The descent of the helicopter felt like an echo of Jodie's heart, which was still sinking as she wondered if the person who had already died was either the bride or groom in that car. She didn't want to do this. It had been hard enough that day when they'd lost the young farmer who had the little boy and a pregnant wife. This was even closer to the bone for Jodie because it involved a couple who had only just married each other. Who were the happiest they'd ever been as they contemplated their new lives together as man and wife. A future built on love and trust and hope.

A future that had just been shattered.

Like it had been for herself and Joel.

Jodie knew she had to pull herself together. There were critically injured patients that might not survive without the help they could get from someone who was absolutely focused on doing what was needed without the distraction that emotion could cause. She knew she could do this. She *had* to do this, but it was going to be the hardest thing she'd ever done.

She caught Eddie's gaze when they were out of the helicopter, their kits on their backs and other equipment in both hands. The scene commander from a major incident police truck was striding towards them and it was only a matter of seconds before this scene would swallow them both for as long as it took.

But Jodie only needed to hold Eddie's gaze for a heartbeat to know that he understood her silent plea.

Stay close. I need you...

Something wasn't right.

Actually, there were so many things that weren't

right that Eddie's senses were being overloaded as he tried to process this scene. The driver of the truck laden with tonnes of rock had slammed sideways into the front half of the stretch limousine, killing the driver of the limousine, probably instantly. The truck driver had been thrown clear as his vehicle tipped sideways, but he had been hit by large rocks spilling from the load and, by the time the air rescue crew had landed, he was also Status Zero.

There were dozens of people milling around a scene bordered by too many damaged cars to count, dressed up in the kind of clothes you wore to weddings with the men in smart suits and the women in colourful dresses with hats or flowers in their hair. There were small girls in puffy white dresses and boys in miniature suits who must have been flower girls and pageboys and a cluster of young women dressed in long, matching pale yellow dresses, one of whom was still clutching a bouquet of flowers. It struck Eddie that this should have been such a happy gathering with those bridesmaids looking like a patch of sunshine, but everyone was looking so shocked and the women wearing yellow were all sobbing and hugging each other. Other people were holding onto the children and some were sitting on the ground or walking around in a dazed fashion, clearly injured, with paramedics moving amongst them.

For Eddie, Jodie and Alex, this was the background of their focus. There were plenty of medics—with more arriving in road crews—to assess and treat the minor to moderate injuries. They were heading to the epicentre of this catastrophe—the wedding car. An ambulance crew was doing CPR on a young man who had been lifted from the wreckage of the car to be laid on a blanket covering flat ground and Eddie's first thought was that a miracle would be needed to get him back from a cardiac arrest caused by any major trauma, but he could see that this patient had suffered a severe head injury as well.

'How long have you been going?'

'Twenty minutes,' someone told Eddie. 'We'll keep going for a bit longer. Right…ready to shock. Stand clear…'

'We need you inside the car,' a senior medic, still coordinating triage of the dozens of people involved in this scene, told Eddie and Jodie. 'The bride's in a bad way too. She was conscious on arrival but her condition's deteriorating rapidly. Chest injuries, query flail chest and she had a major haemorrhage from lacerations to both arms which is under control. Watch out for the broken glass in there.'

'Thanks.' Eddie stepped into the slightly tilted

floor space of the car's interior, slipping off his pack to put to one side as a paramedic stepped back to give him access. He turned back to offer his hand to take Jodie's pack but, to his surprise, she put her hand in his to step up into the crunch of broken glass on metal. This was the woman who was so fiercely independent she automatically refused assistance to even carry a heavy bit of kit but she was gripping his hand for a moment as if it were a lifebelt.

They were both double gloved as protection in an environment with multiple hazards but, for just a heartbeat, it felt to Eddie as though this was skin to skin contact and a part of him felt the ache of missing having Jodie in his life the way she had been only days ago. He'd kept his feelings well hidden over the last few days, though, and he knew that Jodie was grateful that he was making it easier for her, but what was bothering Eddie in this moment was that he had the feeling there was something going on with Jodie that he didn't understand. Something that was linked somehow to her decision that they stopped seeing each other.

Something important?

Yeah…something definitely wasn't right with Jodie. He'd known that ever since they'd got out of the helicopter and he'd got the impression he was seeing something in her eyes that was dark.

Something even more secret than their relationship out of work had been. Something that was threatening enough for Jodie to have triggered a surprisingly powerful protective instinct in Eddie, but there was nothing he could do right now other than hope that Jodie could cope with whatever it was that was bothering her.

It was a huge relief to see the absolute focus coming into her eyes as he felt her letting go of his hand. This was the Jodie Sinclair he was used to seeing—the highly qualified paramedic who was in control of any situation she was faced with and poised to act swiftly to do whatever she could to save a life. He listened to her rapid-fire questions to the medics already there and could almost see the plan of initial interventions forming in her brain as she gathered information about her condition and what injuries had already been noted.

'So she was conscious when you arrived?'

'Only just. Incomprehensible speech and groaning. We had to wait for the firies to cut into the side of the car and then get the other passenger out first. She could squeeze a hand on command but didn't open her eyes. We put her GCS at less than ten. We put in an oropharyngeal airway, put her on high flow oxygen and got an IV line in.'

'What's her heart rate now?'

'One twenty.'

'Respirations?'

'Thirty.' The young paramedic was trying hard to keep up with Jodie's speed.

'Blood pressure?'

'Initially one ten over sixty. Now systolic's ninety and we couldn't get a diastolic.'

'Pulse ox?'

'Currently ninety…no, make that eighty-eight…'

'Okay… I'm going to have a listen to her chest. Keep that mask on her and the oxygen on high flow. Can someone find some shears, please, so we can cut her dress clear?'

Eddie had always been impressed with watching Jodie at work like this. But, right now, he was proud of her as well. He might not know what it was that had threatened her enough to be making this so much more of a challenge, but he did know it would have had to have been something huge to rattle one of the most professional and focused paramedics he'd ever worked with.

The bride's beautifully curled and braided hair framed an unmarked face, but her arms were badly cut by the broken champagne glasses and shards of the bottle she had been thrown into. Her chest must have caught the table holding the champagne bucket and the intricate beading on the bodice of her dress was soaked in blood.

Jodie knelt amongst the bunched-up fabric of the wedding dress as she cut through the heavily beaded bodice with shears to assess her for the kind of injuries that were putting their patient's airway and breathing at imminent risk of failing and then handed the shears to Eddie, who tackled the skirt of the dress. They would need to do a secondary survey as soon as the breathing and airway was controlled, but finding any open long bone fractures or an injured pelvis were part of the primary survey to check for major haemorrhage.

While Jodie was focused on listening to breath sounds, Eddie asked the medics on scene—apart from one who was crouched at the patient's head with a bag mask, keeping the oxygen flow in place and ready to assist her breathing—to step further back to create space as he opened their kits.

'Multiple fractures,' Jodie confirmed as she lifted her hands and then pulled the earpieces of her stethoscope free. 'Chest is hyper-resonant, she's got neck vein distension, she's tachycardic and hypotensive.'

'Tracheal deviation?'

'Can't see any. Yet.'

Jodie caught Eddie's gaze. There were so many possibilities to think of, but the most important right now were a tension pneumothorax or cardiac tamponade from bleeding around the heart. Blunt chest trauma could interfere with the function of the heart and lead to obstructive shock, it could damage coronary arteries and effectively cause a heart attack, or there could be a time bomb waiting in the form of a tear to the aorta, which was the major vessel taking blood from the heart to the rest of the body.

There was nothing they could do to treat an internal injury like that in the back of a crushed car. What they could do, however, was to intubate their patient to control her airway, keep her oxygenated, decompress her chest if an accumulation of blood or air was preventing her breathing and—above all—get her to a major trauma centre and close to an operating theatre as fast as possible. In order to do that, however, they needed to move her out of the wreckage and into a space where they had clear access all around her. If they ran into difficulty securing her airway they would need more pairs of hands, more equipment and the ability to work from any angle.

There was plenty of help to get her onto the stretcher that Alex had placed as near as possible to the car, but it was Jodie and Eddie who prepared for and carried out the rapid sequence intubation, working together as seamlessly and skilfully as they'd been able to do since they'd first met. The gorgeous wedding dress was no more than a pile of discarded, blood-soaked, beaded and embroidered fabric by the time they had the only survivor from the limousine ready for transport—almost hidden by all the monitors they had in place over and around her body. A portable ventilator was doing her breathing for her, there were blood products being infused and every vital sign was being recorded.

She was still alive but Eddie could feel all eyes on them from the crowd of people watching silently. Or almost silently. He heard the grief-stricken cry from a woman who was in the arms of a man and with paramedics and police officers who would have been keeping her updated on what was happening. She was the right age to be a parent of their patient. Or was she the mother of the groom?

The collective grief from all those people was palpable and Eddie saw the way Jodie's glance swerved as they walked past where the new husband's body had been covered with a sheet and was being protected by a police officer. He could see the lines of tension in her face, which could be due to how critical their patient's condition remained, but Eddie knew, deep down, that it was more than that. He'd never seen Jodie less than in control, no matter how critically ill her patient was. It wasn't that she seemed in danger of losing that control now, but her face was pale and tense enough to worry Eddie and the thought that she might be in some kind of trouble was enough to be squeezing his heart so hard that it hurt.

Not that he could allow head space to even think about it right now. They had their work cut out for them to keep this patient alive long enough to hand over to the trauma team already waiting for them in the resuscitation area of the Queen Mother's Hospital in Aberdeen. By the time they accompanied her right into the department, to allow for all monitoring equipment to be changed over, stayed long enough with their handover to see her being rushed up to Theatre and then got back to base and dealt with all the cleaning and restocking that came in the wake of such a big incident, their shift was well over.

Alex had been helping Eddie as the second person to sign off the use and replacement of restricted drugs so it took time to realise he hadn't seen Jodie since she'd taken the cleaned portable ventilator and the defibrillator out to slot back onto their shelf in the helicopter cabin. He wasn't going to head home until he'd seen her, however.

Because he still had that feeling that something wasn't right.

He went upstairs to file his paperwork, to be met by Dion.

'I've had an update from a mate of mine at Police HQ. They've only just cleared the scene after the investigation by the serious crash squad. He wanted to pass on their thanks for your part in what he said was one of the most traumatic accident scenes he's ever been to.'

Eddie swallowed hard. 'It was a rough one.'

Dion put his hand on Eddie's shoulder but his gaze shifted to look down the staircase.

'Is Jodie okay?'

Eddie followed his station manager's gaze to see Jodie sitting in the open door of the helicopter that had been rolled back into the hangar for the night.

Just sitting, with her head bowed and her shoulders hunched.

'I'm not sure,' he answered honestly. 'I'm a bit worried about her.'

'Tell her your patient's got through surgery,' Dion said. 'She's in the ICU. You did well. Both of you.' He gave Eddie's shoulder a squeeze as he let it go. 'And take care of her, will you? You'll be able to do that much better than I can. Take her out for a drink maybe? Talk things through for a debrief?'

Eddie went down the stairs, aware of the irony of having just been given permission to spend time with Jodie away from work when it was something she no longer wanted.

But, as a colleague and a friend, he wasn't about to let her be alone right now.

'Hey…' He walked up to where she was sitting so still. 'Dion tells me that our bride is in ICU. She made it through surgery.'

But the news didn't seem to be welcome. To his horror, Eddie could see the sparkle of tears in Jodie's eyes before she dropped her gaze to avoid his and her voice was no more than a whisper.

'Might have been better if she hadn't.'

Eddie had never seen Jodie this close to tears. He'd never heard such a bleak tone in her voice. It didn't matter that he had Dion's permission to spend time alone with his crewmate. He would have done this anyway.

'You're coming with me,' he told Jodie.

She shook her head. 'I'm going home,' she said. 'I might go for a run.'

Eddie put his finger under her chin so that she was forced to meet his gaze. 'It wasn't an invitation,' he said softly. 'Dion reckons we need a debrief and I agree with him, so I'm just telling you what's going to happen.' He held her gaze. 'You're safe, Jodie. And I'm going to make sure you stay that way.' He let his hand slide down her arm until it reached hers and then he pulled her to her feet and then into a hug. It didn't matter that Dion was probably still watching them. His lips were against her ear. 'Maybe I need this as much as you do. So you're coming with me, okay?'

He felt rather than heard Jodie's response as her head moved slowly against his shoulder. Up and down.

Okay...

Eddie glanced up as he led the way out of the hangar and he saw Dion was also nodding as he turned away. The older man probably assumed they'd be heading for the Pig and Thistle—maybe with Alex and Gus for a full crew debrief—but Eddie was quite certain that Jodie needed a far more private space than that.

She needed protection, and that was something he wasn't about to let anyone or anything prevent him providing.

CHAPTER NINE

IT WASN'T THAT cold this evening, but Jodie seemed frozen to the point where it seemed like it was too difficult to even move her facial muscles enough to talk.

So Eddie didn't ask any questions.

He lit the gas fire in the small living room/ kitchen area of his apartment and, when that didn't seem enough, he pulled the duvet from his bed and wrapped it around Jodie as she sat, hunched, on his couch.

He made her a mug of hot, sweet tea and, when that didn't seem enough, he added a slug of his favourite whisky. He made one for himself as well and sat beside her as he sipped the drink.

It was Jodie who broke what was actually becoming a rather companionable silence.

'It's Saturday night. Don't you have something better to do than sit at home like this?'

'Nope.' Eddie shook his head. 'I probably would have gone to visit my brother, Mick, but I know my other brother, James, was coming up today so I can catch up with them both tomorrow.'

'How's he doing? Mick, I mean…'

Eddie drained his mug. 'Not great. He's not eating properly and he's losing weight. He goes through the motions of doing his therapy but it's kind of half-hearted and any progress has stalled. It's like he lost a much bigger part of himself in that accident than just the ability to walk. My sister Ella's thinking we might have to think about a family intervention of some kind.'

'Like what?'

'She and her husband have found this idyllic-looking rehab centre in New Zealand. They want to go there for a belated honeymoon and they've got this idea of taking Mick and putting him somewhere different for a month or two. Somewhere gorgeous and warm with forests and a beach that's safe enough to take disabled people swimming in the sea. He says he doesn't want to go because he'd be a burden for all that travelling, but she says maybe they should just take him anyway.'

'Does he have a wife? Or a partner?'

'No.' Eddie let his breath out in a wry huff of sound. 'He fell in love enough to want to marry a rather gorgeous Brazilian woman who told him she was pregnant with his baby a few years back. James and I were right beside him at the altar as his best men on his wedding day—waiting for the bride who never showed up.'

Jodie was silent for a moment and then her voice was very quiet. 'Had *she* had an accident? On the way to the church?'

'The only accident she had was to get pregnant,' Eddie muttered. 'The real father of the baby had turned up and that was that. They were off to live happily ever after together and Mick was thoroughly and very publicly jilted. He vowed he'd never make the mistake of committing himself to any woman after that and he persuaded me and James to join in the pact. We needed to learn from his example and never try to get married. Life was short and we all needed to live hard. Mick took the rules a bit more seriously than we did, mind you. I've never felt the urge to jump off a cliff to go hang-gliding.' Eddie stopped as he remembered the first moment he'd ever set eyes on Jodie, in the staffroom that morning, when she'd been declaring that the best thing ever was to jump off the side of a mountain with just a small parachute to keep you alive. He lifted his mug and then remembered it was empty. 'Want a top-up?' he asked Jodie.

She held out her mug. 'Yes, please...'

Eddie busied himself in the kitchen for a few minutes and when he carried the fresh mugs of spiked tea back to the couch he found Jodie still snuggled into the duvet like a caterpillar in a cocoon, but she didn't have that frozen look to her face any longer. Her lips were a much better colour as well.

He handed her a mug and then held his up to touch it. 'Cheers,' he said.

But Jodie just nodded and then took a long sip of her tea.

'I get it,' she said, a moment later. 'I get what Mick gets out of doing that dangerous stuff.'

'The adrenaline rush?'

'It's bigger than that when you lose something that's really important. For me, it started when I wasn't that bothered about whether or not I was going to survive the jump. It was like throwing myself into the hands of fate. If I got caught, I survived—and maybe that would mean there was a reason to keep going.'

Eddie's breath caught in his chest.

'What did you lose?' he asked quietly.

'The love of my life.'

Wow... There wasn't anything Eddie could think of to say. That was about as important as it got, wasn't it? No wonder he'd been so certain that Jodie couldn't be 'the one' for him, or rather that he wasn't *her* soul mate. She had already had one. At least he could put his arm around Jodie as her friend, and she seemed to like that because she leaned against him.

'I met Joel when we started high school together,' Jodie continued softly. 'We were friends from the first day and we started dating when we were fourteen. We never even thought about dating anyone else. We took a gap year when we left school because we wanted to travel to as many places as we possibly could before we settled down and went to university and got good jobs and then started having kids.'

Jodie wasn't looking at him, so Eddie tightened his hold on her just a little and made a sound that let her know he was listening to every word she was saying. That he knew this was important and that she had more to say. He wanted to hear that too.

If felt like he *needed* to hear it.

'We got as far as Bali,' Jodie said. 'And it was so beautiful and we were so happy that we decided to get married. On the beach. As soon as we could. I bought a pretty white dress at a market and had my toenails painted with tiny white daisies on them. I think the most expensive thing we bought was a gorgeous bunch of gardenias that I was going to carry. Joel bought a cheap white shirt at the market, but he wore it with his shorts that were bright blue—as blue as the sea and the sky the day we got married. He went swimming in them later that day in the sunset… I just went in as far I could without getting my dress wet while I was holding it up because I didn't want to ruin it. I wanted to keep it for ever and wear it on every anniversary…'

The silence was heavy this time. Jodie had her eyes closed.

'My dress got ruined anyway,' she finally said, in a broken whisper. 'I was kneeling on the beach in the dark, hours later, when they finally found where the rip had taken him and brought him back to put in my arms. I couldn't move, even when the waves broke all around us.'

There were tears rolling down Jodie's cheeks now and Eddie's heart was breaking right around her like those waves on her tragic wedding day. He understood her words that it might have better if the bride they'd gone to today hadn't survived after losing the man she had just married. Jodie knew the agony she had ahead of her.

How hard must it have been for Jodie to have coped with that scene?

It was instinctive to reach for her with his other arm as well. To enfold her and hold her close. To brush away the tears on her face and pull her tight against his chest as she cried. He was crying himself, but part of that emotion was because he knew he was holding the most extraordinary woman he'd ever met. Someone courageous enough to pick up the pieces of her broken life and make something totally awesome out of it.

Someone who had, today, faced up to what must have brought back the worst memories she could have and she had been able to put them aside in order to help someone else.

Someone who deserved every bit of the love and happiness she had dreamed of having in her life.

In her sadness, Jodie felt smaller than he remembered her being in his arms. Vulnerable. Eddie bent his head and pressed a kiss against the tousled waves of her hair. He felt her head move beneath his lips but he hadn't expected the way she raised her face so that *her* lips touched his.

And then they were kissing each other and Eddie could feel Jodie's need that was almost desperation. Was it a need for him? Or did she simply need human contact and an affirmation of life?

It didn't matter.

Jodie needed this and he could give it to her and that was the only thing that mattered. He scooped up the whole bundle of duvet with her inside it and carried it to his bed.

It was the last thing Jodie would have planned to happen after a rough day at work. The last thing she would have thought she wanted.

But it turned out that it was exactly what she needed.

Being held like this. Not being alone under that comforting layer of the warm duvet. Being naked so that she could feel the warmth of Eddie's skin against hers and the touch of his fingertips and hands as they moved over her body, making her skin tingle.

Making her so aware that she was still alive.

Gentle enough to make her feel cared for. Cherished, even.

She was the one who pushed things into a demand. For something harder and faster and challenging enough to be almost a battle.

So that she could be aware of winning? To remind herself that she could still be in control?

To remember that she was a survivor.

That she was lucky enough to be able to appreciate the good things that life had to offer. Like this...the comfort of touch. That sharp pull of desire and the delicious, if brief, dip into ecstasy that made the rest of the world fade for as long as it lasted.

She would continue to survive, Jodie thought as she lay in Eddie's arms with only the sound of his breath in the air around her and the thump of his heart beneath her cheek. She would carry on with what had become her passion in life as well. She might not be able to win every time. Nobody could have saved the young groom today and there was no way anyone could prevent the struggle that his bride was going to face if she won her battle for her life, but Jodie knew she had made a difference and who knew how many other lives she would be able to save in the future?

She propped herself up on her elbow. 'I'm not sure Dion would approve of that debrief,' she said.

One side of Eddie's mouth curled upwards. 'Dion won't know anything about it.'

'No.'

'The only thing he'll want to know is that you're okay.'

Jodie nodded. Thanks to Eddie, she was. But then she caught her bottom lip between her teeth.

'I don't want anyone else to know,' she told him. 'About what I told you? About Joel? I don't want anyone trying to second-guess how well I'm going to cope at a difficult scene. Or keep me from doing my job.'

'I would never betray a confidence,' Eddie said. 'But nobody's ever going to stop you doing your job. You coped as well as anyone could have today. Better than most. I knew something was bothering you, but I could see the moment you shut it down and just got on with it. And…' Eddie touched her face softly '…knowing what I do now makes me realise just how strong a person you are. You're amazing, Jodie.'

Jodie pulled away from his touch. She sat up and then leaned over the side of the bed to pick up some of her clothing.

'I have to go,' she said, pulling her tee shirt over her head without bothering to put her bra back on. She was about to swing her legs out of the bed, but she paused and turned to catch Eddie's gaze.

'I'm glad you know,' she said. 'Because it means you understand why I can't do this again. Why *we* can't do this again. Why I don't do relationships. I... I like you too much, Eddie, but I'm not going to let myself fall in love with you and the easiest way to stop that happening is to stop *this* happening.'

Eddie's gaze softened. 'I get it,' he said quietly. 'You've experienced such a devastating loss that you never want to go through that again.'

Jodie shook her head. 'It's not that I don't *want* to go through it again. You make it sound like a choice. I *can't* go through it again. It was a loss that made my world stop turning and, if it happened again, I'd never be able to get it started a second time.'

This time, she did get out of bed to get the rest of her clothes on.

'You don't do relationships because you made some kind of pact with your brothers when one of you had been burned by a bad relationship that was obviously never genuine on both sides and you'd probably all had far too much to drink.'

Eddie made a face. 'You're not completely off the mark, there.'

'It's not a good enough reason.' Jodie felt her heart break a little as she looked back. 'I *really* like you, Eddie, and you deserve more than just skating through life on a superficial level, having sex that doesn't mean anything.' Her voice wobbled. 'You deserve someone who can give you a hell of a lot more than I could. You deserve to find out what love is really about and…and that's never going to be with me and that's why this is never going to happen again. Okay…?'

It wasn't a question. Any more than Eddie's had been when he was telling her that she was going to go with him so that he could look after her.

Because he cared that much about her.

Jodie didn't even stay in Eddie's room long enough to give him the chance to respond. Maybe she cared too much about him too.

Maybe that was why this was a lot harder than she had expected it to be.

Perhaps it was a good thing that it was never going to happen again.

Because that last time with Jodie was already haunting Eddie. He'd been thinking about her when he'd finally fallen asleep just before dawn and she was his first waking thought when he became conscious again.

Texting her was not pushing any boundaries she might not want him to cross, was it? It was something friends could do?

You okay?

He sent the text before he had time to talk himself out of it.

The response was immediate.

I'm good. Just off for a run. Might go hiking up the Cairngorms tomorrow and get a look at where we're going to that abseiling course.

Oh… The fact that she was okay thinking about time they would have together on that course was enough for Eddie to breathe a sigh of relief. He wanted to suggest he went with her but he knew that would not be a good idea—for either of them.

Instead, he sent:

Keep an eye out for snow. I might need another pair of those pink pants.

He received a 'thumbs-up' emoji back, but the text came in at the same time as another one and, as Eddie read Ella's message, he realised he couldn't have gone out of the city for the day anyway, because it seemed their concerns about Mick had suddenly escalated into a crisis. Their brother had apparently stopped eating altogether and was avoiding talking to anyone by pretending to be asleep.

Even as Eddie drove to the rehab centre as soon as he was up and dressed, he was still thinking about Jodie.

About last night.

Of course it had been different, he told himself. They'd had a really rough day being part of the horror when a joyous wedding party turned into an unthinkable tragedy that was going to impact so many lives. And Jodie, with the echo of her own tragedy, had been through an emotional maelstrom that had made their time together seem far more significant than it really had been. No wonder it had taken the sex to another level.

One that made it feel it was more like touching souls than merely parts of their physical bodies.

Was that the kind of connection that Jodie had had with Joel? The love of her life that she had no intention of even trying to replace? Eddie found himself wondering what it would be like to be loved so hard that the world would stop turning if something happened to him.

The only people he'd ever felt a bond like that

with were his siblings, especially the brothers he'd been so close to even before they knew each other existed. There were times when they felt like one being that had been split into three parts and the worry that he was driving towards a real test of whether that bond could ever be broken was finally enough for Eddie to let Jodie go.

From his personal life? For ever?

No. That was never going to happen. Not on a really personal level because he was never going to forget what it was like to be that close to Jodie Sinclair and he knew he was never going to find anyone remotely like her again. She'd said she wasn't going to allow herself to fall in love with him—as if it was something that was possible to control? Eddie wasn't so sure about that.

Because he was starting to wonder if he had already fallen in love with *her*.

What he could do, however, was to stop himself thinking about her this much. For now, anyway. He knew she was okay and coping in her own way with her passion for physical activities. And Eddie had more urgent matters to focus on that could well fill all the days off before he would be anywhere near Jodie again.

As a family, the Grishams—and Logan—gathered around Mick, spending time with him individually and together, with and without the support of the rehabilitation centre's psychologists and therapists. It was another emotional rollercoaster for Eddie, but it did make it easier to have something so important to deal with that it was actually possible to stop thinking about Jodie during his days and he was so exhausted by the time he fell into bed at night that he was asleep almost instantly.

This crisis with Mick was important—and personal enough—to stop him feeling weirdly envious of a ghost.

Envious of anyone, even, who had a partner in life who loved them that much. He watched his sister being wrapped in her husband's arms in a moment when they thought they were unobserved and the strength of their love for each other was enough to bring a lump to his throat.

He wanted that for himself one day.

And while he could understand why, he still felt sad for Jodie that she would never allow herself to feel like that again about anyone else.

Okay…he felt sad for himself too. That he couldn't be the one who could fill that gap in her life, but that was going to have to be a secret. Even more of a secret than the stolen hours he and Jodie had spent together because that had been a shared secret.

How he was feeling now was entirely his own.

* * *

When Mick responded to the deep concern of the people who loved *him* the most and agreed to go along with the plan his family had suggested, Eddie's days suddenly became far too busy to think about anything or anyone else. Ella and Logan had already booked their honeymoon. James was already planning to start his locum position in Aberdeen's Queen Mother's hospital. With Mick agreeing to try a visit to the exclusive treatment centre in New Zealand, and extensive online interviews with the medical teams involved on both sides of the world before the New Zealand centre agreed to take him, there were suddenly what felt like a million things to get organised and chaos was lurking around every corner.

Airlines had to be contacted in person to plead for last-minute seats and the special assistance that would be needed. Ella and Logan took care of the medical side of caring for Mick on such a long journey, taking supplies for any contingency they could think of. A new wheelchair had to be sourced that was suitable for travelling and patient records copied and filed. James was due to move so he had to pack his flat up in Edinburgh so he could sublet it and he had too much to shift up to Ella and Logan's place with only a motorbike for transport so Eddie made a couple of trips south with his SUV to help.

On his last day off he helped with taking everybody and their huge amount of luggage to the airport and stood side by side with James as they watched Mick being taken onto his flight that would connect with the long-haul journey to New Zealand. Eddie had helped bring one of his brothers even closer to where he was building his new life but he was sending the other to the far side of the planet at exactly the same time and...

And it felt weird. As if the fabric of his life was being pulled apart all over again. Not with the painful rip that Mick's accident had created but in a sense that puzzle pieces were being juggled because they didn't fit where they'd been placed so it was time to try something new.

For all of them.

Thank goodness it didn't feel weird to be back at work. If anything, the potential awkwardness of being crewed with someone he'd had an off-limits sexual relationship with seemed to have been burnt off by the emotional overload both he and Jodie had been through in the last few days.

A time that had been intense enough to have generated thoughts and feelings that were over the top. Like thinking that he'd fallen in love with Jodie? Eddie was grateful for the filter of emotional exhaustion that allowed him to find a reality that would be much easier to live with than the secret angst of a very immature unrequited love.

This felt like a genuine friendship between himself and Jodie now. One with a foundation that was rock solid because they shared a secret that only the two of them knew.

Two secrets, in fact.

Eddie would never dream of breaking Jodie's trust by sharing the very private information of the tragedy she'd had to deal with in her past. And he knew that Jodie was not about to confess to anyone how close she and Eddie had become while they'd sorted out that small issue of how attracted they'd been to each other.

That was in the past too.

Hopefully, Jodie felt the same way he did and didn't regret any of it. Because it had generated a personal level of trust that could have taken decades to build in an ordinary kind of friendship. Add that to the professional level of trust they had been building on since they'd first worked together and it was something very special indeed. While he might not have fallen *in* love with her, Eddie cared about Jodie very much and that was a more than acceptable form of love between good friends.

Hey…it would probably last a lot longer than any other kind, wouldn't it?

Good news arrived a couple of days later, that Mick was safely at his new rehab centre in New Zealand after the long journey had been completed without any complications. Ella had sent Eddie a photograph of him meeting his personal therapist, Riley, who was none other than the blonde woman with the beautiful smile who'd featured on the rehab centre's webpage.

Eddie smiled and forwarded the photo to James. 'Lucky man' he added as a caption.

He was even luckier, though, wasn't he?

Eddie was fit and healthy. He had a job he loved and a crew to work with that was absolutely the best. He had a friendship that was going to last a lifetime if he had any say in the matter and, as a bonus, he was going to get out into the mountains and spend a couple of days with that friend doing something new and exciting. He couldn't wait.

CHAPTER TEN

WAS THIS WHAT real happiness felt like?

Being out in nature in a place so beautiful it was a constant reminder of how lucky she was to be alive?

Floor-to-ceiling windows in this unexpectedly gorgeous lodge afforded stunning mountain views against a clear blue sky and even included a glimpse of a waterfall above the forests surrounding the river and this outdoor recreation centre. Declan—one of the instructors for the abseiling course both Jodie and Eddie were attending this weekend—told them in the meet and greet that, if they were confident enough, they could be doing their more advanced outside sessions tomorrow close to the dramatic curtains of water that the falls created in the cliffs. Today, however, along with some real beginners to abseiling, they would be playing on some smaller crags that were less intimidating.

Eddie caught Jodie's glance and grinned. Then he leaned closer so that only she could hear him.

'Dream come true for me,' he whispered. 'I've always wanted to get up close and personal with a waterfall.'

The first session was indoors and covered information that was already more than familiar for both Jodie and Eddie with the knowledge and experience they'd gained, both through their rescue winch training and their now shared hobby of bouldering, but their attendance here was partly a box-ticking exercise that would allow them to get accreditation with the organisation that provided International Rope Access qualifications and then move on to more advanced levels. If nothing else, it promised to be a fun weekend out in the kind of environment they both loved.

Who wouldn't be happy?

'Putting aside our personal protective equipment like helmets and gloves,' Declan said, 'these are the two vital elements that you could not abseil without. A rope and a harness. We'll get into the carabiners and belay devices that are the interfaces between the two very soon but let's start with this.' He picked up an item from the top of one of the closest piles on the floor of this lounge.

'This is a basic harness. Sorry, Eddie and Jodie—they're not up to the standard you guys will be used to, with all the bells and whistles for attachments, but they're all we need for what we're going to be doing.' He held the harness up by the largest loop. 'This loop goes around your waist and the two loops underneath go around your legs and there's a loop on the front which is where your belay device will be attached. We want to get you all into one that's fitting well and is comfortable. We'll come around and help. Maybe Jodie and Eddie can give you a hand as well, when they've got their own harnesses on.'

Jodie saw Eddie from the corner of her eye a minute or two later, adjusting the buckles on the leg loops of a harness a young woman was wearing and Jodie actually fumbled with one of the buckles she was working with herself to help someone else. It was as if she could *feel* the brush of Eddie's fingers against the top of her own legs. She could certainly feel the tingle of sensation that pooled low in her body, but it wasn't desire, she reminded herself. It was a memory and Jodie was finding that she could not only deal with it but perhaps even learn to embrace it.

Okay…if she was honest, she was really missing the intimate part of what they'd had together but, if that was the price for keeping her world under control and safe, then she was prepared to pay it. No. As she'd told Eddie on that last, poignant night they'd had alone together, it wasn't a choice at all. It was simply something she had to do in order to survive.

That spiral of sensation was another reminder that she was alive and could experience pleasure from her body as well as her environment and the anticipation of a challenge—as long as she could keep within the safety barriers she was busy rebuilding. And, if she was honest, it had to be adding a bit of spice to the way she was feeling.

Eddie, bless him, was still making this transition easy so it was beginning to seem like they might be lucky enough that they could end up being friends with none of the awkwardness that usually came when people took a friendship too far and then tried to dial it back.

So yeah...

This felt like a level of happiness that was the most Jodie could ever expect—or allow—if she was going to keep herself safe, so she was going to make the most of this weekend.

She couldn't help another glance in Eddie's direction, though, and, as if he'd felt it, he looked across the room, one eyebrow raised just enough to make it a question.

You okay? You enjoying this?

Jodie smiled back. Holding his gaze felt so natural. Weirdly, being able to feel that dimension to their friendship that should have made it harder to be around Eddie was making her feel even safer. Because she trusted him completely and she knew he cared enough about her to want her to be safe. And happy.

She could feel her smile widen into a message that Eddie wouldn't be able to miss.

I'm loving it...

She looked...happy.

Being in Jodie's company and sharing a good time that was making her this happy was... well...it was the best that Eddie could hope for, wasn't it?

Exactly what he had always wanted to be able to have with any woman he'd been attracted to enough to get closer than simply a friend or colleague, after the need to step back from expectations of it becoming something more. He was getting a masterclass in how to be the perfect playboy, in fact, which would have been very useful a decade or more ago. Given that he'd known what he was signing up for right from the get-go, he should be just as happy as Jodie was with the way things were going. And he would be, he told himself firmly, as soon as he got used to this new normal.

They moved onto ropes after everyone was wearing a secure harness.

'These are at the thicker end for the size of

climbing ropes,' Declan told them. 'That makes them run slower through the belay device and gives you better control over your speed. We're going to practise tying some knots now and top of that list is the Prusik friction knot. It's this knot that will be your safety mechanism and stop you falling, so it's important. When we've mastered that, we can head outside and you can have some fun on some real rocks.'

It took a while, because most people were struggling to assimilate the information and techniques about unfamiliar knots but, with a smile here and a quick glance there, Eddie and Jodie were soon quietly having a bit of a race to see who could do the fastest and neatest coiling and tying of the practice lengths of rope. And it was fun.

Was this his own safety mechanism for being with Jodie? Doing something challenging enough to need focus? Eddie already knew that professional boundaries kept things safe at work, but how good would it be to enjoy time together out of work like this without being blindsided by the occasional flash of the kind of pain—or was it sadness?—that came from thinking something huge had been lost for ever?

Yeah…the challenge and fun of the hours spent outside for the rest of the day made Eddie confident that this new normal could work. It helped that Declan divided the group early on that afternoon so that he and Jodie could do some more intensive training.

'We'll sort out a programme for completing all levels of the accreditation course tomorrow and maybe you can book in to come and stay here again.'

'Sounds like a plan.' Jodie nodded. 'I'd be up for that. What about you, Eddie?'

There was almost a plea in the glance Eddie received. Could they do this? Together? Have a real friendship and maybe stay in each other's lives for ever? Eddie had a strong misgiving that trying to do that might hold him back from ever moving on from being with Jodie but he made sure he sounded enthusiastic. Fake it till you make it, right?

'Count me in,' he agreed.

Maybe it was because he was physically tired by the end of the afternoon sessions that it got more difficult to be near Jodie. Maybe the echo of that misgiving was doing its best to put down roots. Or perhaps it was the thought, as evening fell, that they were both going to be sleeping under the same roof but in different beds that tipped the balance.

Whatever the cause, by the time dinner was over, Eddie wasn't feeling nearly as happy as he had been. Cell phone coverage was dismal in this mountainous area so he couldn't distract himself by messaging his family to catch up on how Mick was, whether Ella and Logan had rented a camper van yet or if James had had any interesting cases coming through his new emergency department at Queen's. He didn't want to go and join Jodie where she was helping other members of the group who wanted to practise their knots again because that certainly wasn't going to silence that niggling thought at the back of his mind that he was only making things worse by trying to convince himself that a friendship with Jodie was going to be enough.

That the sensible thing to do would be to create some distance. Not just tonight but back at work as well. It might even help if he had a quiet word with Dion and got himself shifted to a different crew? In the past, in a situation like this, Eddie would have simply packed up and moved to another job. Another country. He would have found a fresh start and, he was a bit ashamed to admit it but it was the truth—he would have found a new friendship with the kind of benefits that would have been more than enough of a distraction. But he couldn't do that this time. And it wasn't just because of that wakeup call that had made him want a more meaningful relationship and commitment in his life.

He was in this difficult space in his head because of the same reason he was in this new city and new job. There were things in life that were too important not to commit to. Discovering that coming back to his homeland of Scotland had made Eddie feel like he was where he truly belonged in the world was a bonus, but he had come back for his family. He was living in the same city as his brother James for the first time in years and Mick's absence was temporary. He'd come back, hopefully ready to make his own commitment to embrace life again, and Eddie needed to be here to support him.

So he couldn't leave Aberdeen. He couldn't leave his job. Relationships with family—and hopefully a partner—might be at the top of his list of important things in life but his career wasn't just a job, it was a major part of who he was. Stepping away from air rescue to work on a road crew felt like it would be a step too far, but creating a bit of distance by being in a different crew and working opposing shifts on the air rescue base seemed like an option that could work.

But what could he say to Dion? That he was sorry he'd broken the rules? That he'd been stupid to think that it would be no problem to have one last superficial, just-for-fun hook-up with a gorgeous woman but it was never going to happen again? And no harm had been done. The attraction had been mutual but it was over and done with? End of story—for both of them?

No. He couldn't do that because it would get Jodie into a whole heap of trouble. He probably couldn't even make it sound convincing when he wasn't sure he believed it himself.

And what about that misgiving that had the real potential to start growing like a weed?

How on earth was he supposed to find the person he wanted to be with for the rest of his life when he was still this close to Jodie? When, deep down, he knew it would be impossible to find anyone he wanted to be with as much as he still wanted to be with Jodie Sinclair.

Oh, man... He needed to clear his head.

He picked up his anorak and walked over to where Declan was having a coffee with the other instructors.

'I'm just going to get a bit of fresh air,' he told them.

'Got a torch? The moon might be out now but it could disappear any time.'

'Yeah...' Eddie put the band of the forehead torch over his head.

'Stick to the tracks,' Declan advised. 'And don't go too far, okay? You'll want a good night's sleep so you're ready for tomorrow's challenges.'

Eddie smiled and nodded, but he lengthened his stride as soon as he got outside the lodge.

If he was going to get any sleep at all tonight he would have to deal with the conflict going on in his head and that was clearly going to take more than just a bit of a stroll.

Jodie could feel Eddie's absence before she could see that he wasn't in the lounge or dining area of the lodge any longer.

'Did Eddie go to bed?' she asked Declan when he joined the group to offer to put a documentary about abseiling on the wide screen television.

'No. He went outside for some fresh air. He should be back any time now—I told him not to go too far.'

There was no real reason for Jodie to wander outside to see if she could see him returning. There was probably every reason why she shouldn't, but it was impossible to focus on the documentary, despite its amazing scenery and photography.

Something didn't feel right and...and it was something important enough to feel urgent.

She slipped out of the room, found her warm jacket and torch and went outside, following the main track they had used earlier today that led uphill from the lodge. She kept expecting to see Eddie coming downhill around the next corner but she began wondering if he'd even taken this track at all, until she cleared the main band of forest that gave way to areas of bare rock at the base of cliffs. She could see a flicker of light above her that had to be Eddie's head torch.

She could also hear how much louder the background sound of the river was and that was when she remembered what Eddie had whispered in her ear this morning.

'I've always wanted to get up close and personal with a waterfall...'

He had to know that going alone at this time of night was far from sensible. It was out of character for Eddie to be taking a risk like this, no matter how confident in his abilities he might have felt. Jodie was going to tell him exactly how stupid he'd been, in no uncertain terms, as soon as she caught up with him.

Rehearsing what she was going to say only made her feel increasingly worried and she pushed herself to go faster. The next time she saw the light it was a lot closer.

'Eddie...' She had to yell to get heard above the sound of water crashing onto rock. *'Stop...* Wait for me...'

The light got brighter as if he'd turned his head at the sound of her voice. Then she heard his voice. It was faint but she could tell it wasn't calling her name. He wasn't saying any words.

It sounded like a cry of astonishment.

Or fear...?

And then the light was snuffed out as if a switch had been flicked.

He'd fallen.

Jodie knew that.

She just didn't know how bad it was. Maybe she would hear him calling for help, or better yet—see his light again any second as he got to his feet and kept coming down the track.

But that wasn't stopping a fear that was turning her blood to ice in her veins.

Eddie could have fallen too close to the edge of the waterfall and been swept away. He could have been smashed against rocks and knocked unconscious. Or he might be trapped below the surface by the force of the water pounding into a deep pool.

Oh, dear Lord…he might be *drowning*…

A broken sob broke from Jodie's throat. No… that sound and pain was really coming from a very different place.

Her heart…

Her soul…

All those safety barriers she'd built up so very carefully over the years were totally useless, weren't they? They'd been swept away as easily as if that waterfall had picked them up and made them vanish into nothing more solid than a fine spray of liquid. She'd been lulled into a false sense of security over the years simply because she'd met the person who could change everything.

She hadn't seen it coming or recognised it at the time but she'd never actually been safe from the first moment she'd met Edward Grisham.

She loved him. Just as much as she'd ever loved Joel. More, perhaps, because this was strong enough to have annihilated those protective barriers. She might have denied it so effectively she hadn't realised it was happening, but that day at the fundraising event when she'd felt that yearning to be a part of Eddie's future—to be holding his baby in her arms, even—had been a sure sign that she'd lost any protection she'd thought she had. No wonder she'd panicked and backed off. But how had she believed she was back in control? That she'd never be in this particular space ever again, with her world in danger of slamming to a halt so devastatingly she'd never be able to start it turning again.

'*Dammit*, Eddie…' Jodie's words were choked. By unbearable emotion and the fact that she was so out of breath it felt as if her body was on fire. She was forced to stop and bend over, her hands on her knees as she struggled to get enough oxygen to take the pain from her muscles and allow her lungs to function adequately again.

She was close enough to the river for the rushing water to be a constant background sound. Straightening, Jodie pushed closer, to find a dark, deep pool, surrounded by enormous boulders with a small waterfall that was catching the moonlight enough to make it shimmer as it foamed down the vertical drop from the ledge of rock about five metres above Jodie. This wasn't the waterfall they could see from the lodge windows because that one had to be over a thirty-metre drop and the big one would have been what Eddie was heading towards, wouldn't it?

He didn't do anything by halves.

Except...

Jodie was still looking up at the lip of the ledge the water was flowing over so smoothly and she saw something in the trees to one side of it. A glowing spot that was too bright to be swallowed by the moonlight. A shape that had to be manmade.

'*Eddie*...' Jodie had to clear the lump from her throat and try again. '*Eddie*...? Can you hear me?'

'*Jodie?*'

The spot of light moved. Disappeared and then appeared again, right beside where the water started its drop. It was too dark to see Eddie's face beneath the bright bulb of the torch but Jodie could sense every one of his features. Those dark eyes, that strong nose...those lips that could curve into the most delicious smile in the entire world...

The relief that he was not only alive but conscious and moving was enough for tears to be streaming down Jodie's face and her voice was raw.

'Oh, my God, Eddie... Are you hurt?'

'I don't think so... Maybe a bit. I tripped and went into a slide and bumped a few rocks on the way. I landed in the water but managed to catch a tree branch before I went over the top. I can't get close enough to see... Can I climb down to where you are?'

Jodie scanned the rock face on either side of the waterfall. It was almost sheer but, with her practised eye, she could pick out the variations in contour and texture that could provide grip or support for hands and feet, although that would still be risky with how wet the wall was from the waterfall's spray.

'No way,' she called. 'Even going up would be a challenge. If you fell and didn't land in the pool, you'd kill yourself. I'd kind of prefer that you didn't do that.'

What an understatement. But Jodie was still grappling with the realisation that she was head over heels, heart and soul in love with Eddie and that was too huge to even think about putting into words. She pulled out her phone but had to watch helplessly as two bars on her phone went to one and then reception cut out completely before she could even try calling for help.

'I'll try climbing back up to the track, then...' Eddie shouted. The torchlight swerved and hit the trees again. And then, to Jodie's horror, it faded, flickered and went out.

She heard Eddie's groan of frustration. 'I think my batteries are dead. But maybe I can... I could...'

The sudden short silence from above turned into another groan that made Jodie catch her breath.

'What's wrong?'

'I... I'm a bit dizzy, that's all.'

'Did you bump your head in that fall?'

'I don't know. I don't remember...'

Jodie saw the dark shape that was Eddie's head disappear. Was he lying down? Losing consciousness? Confused enough to think it might be a good idea to try climbing back to the track without even torchlight to guide him?

'*Eddie?*'

There was no response.

'Don't move,' Jodie yelled. 'I'm coming up.'

She had no choice. Yes, she knew it was dangerous, but she couldn't stay here and not know whether Eddie was okay. She knew she should go for help but she couldn't go in the opposite direction to where Eddie was. The need to be close to him—to be able to *touch* him—was the only thing filling her mind.

It wasn't as if she didn't know what she was doing and the first few metres were easy. The faults in the rock were almost like steps and there were plenty of hand grips. But then her fingers started getting colder and it was harder to see whether it was safe to stretch towards a new hold or if the light from her torch was creating shadows that were illusions of a protrusion or gap that wouldn't actually be able to take her weight. The darkness outside the circle of light from her torch made things so much worse. She couldn't see how far she'd come up but it felt like a yawning chasm beneath her that would swallow her instantly if she fell. She couldn't see how far it was to the top either and, at one point, she froze—glued to the wall like a spider, unable to see how to get higher but knowing it would be impossible to turn back. There was only one direction she could go, despite her feet aching so badly and her fingers beginning to go numb.

She could only ever go towards Eddie…

And, unexpectedly, as she reached up to skim her hand against the rock to try and locate a handhold, she felt herself caught by a strong grip around her wrist. Eddie was leaning over the edge. He scrunched his eyes closed as she tilted her head up and blinded him with her torchlight but his voice was as strong as his grip.

'I've got you, sweetheart. You can do this...'

Sweetheart...

He'd called her sweetheart for the first time—the first person to ever call her that—and the endearment filled her heart and then wrapped itself around her entire body like a hug as she used the safety of his grip as a hold and pushed herself up towards him.

And then she was in his arms and she could hear him telling her that she was safe and that everything was going to be okay, but Jodie was sobbing. And...angry...

She was *so* angry.

She pushed herself back and didn't care that he had to shade his eyes from the glare of the beam of light on her head.

'This is all your fault,' she shouted through her tears. 'It shouldn't have happened.'

'I know, I'm sorry...' Eddie tried to wrap his arms around her but she was pushing back hard with her fists. 'But it'll be okay. I promise. I'm not hurt. *You're* not hurt. Declan knows I'm out here, and they're probably already on their way to find us, and—'

But Jodie was shaking her head. 'I'm not talking about *this*. I'm talking about falling in love with you. I told you I couldn't do this again...that

I couldn't ever let myself love someone enough to make losing them the end of the world and… and now it's happened and…and I'm scared because I have no idea what to do about it…'

All the fight suddenly drained out of Jodie and she closed her eyes, feeling her body go completely limp—surrendering to being folded into Eddie's arms and held against his chest.

He was still making reassuring sounds and his voice was so clear because it was right beside her ear, so close she could feel the warmth of his breath.

'It's not a problem,' he was telling her. 'I promise… Because I *do* know exactly what to do about it.'

She looked up. 'How? What…?'

Eddie pressed the button that turned off her torch. For a heartbeat or two Jodie couldn't see anything at all due to the sudden change in light, but then she found she could see Eddie's face in the moonlight. She could see his eyes. And his smile.

'Because I love you that much too,' he told her. 'And I know how scary it is. If I lost you it would feel like way too much of my world was ending as well. That's why I had to try and be happy to just be your friend, even though I knew it would never be enough.'

'So what are we supposed to do? I thought

I could protect myself from it ever happening again, but that didn't work out so well, did it?'

'We're going to protect each other,' Eddie said, simply.

'How can we do that?'

'We can love each other. For as long as we're lucky enough to have together.'

'You make it sound so easy.'

'Maybe it is when you don't have a choice. When, you know…you kind of want the world to keep turning.'

Jodie's last coherent thought, as Eddie's lips covered hers in the most amazing kiss that had ever been bestowed, was that maybe he was right.

Didn't someone even say that once? That love made the world go round?

The kiss couldn't last, of course, but that didn't matter because Jodie knew there would be an infinite number of kisses to come. And hearing the calls of people coming to find them was the first step back to safety. Back to where her life was going to start all over again.

With Eddie.

He turned on her head torch and they heard the shout of delight from the searchers.

'There you are, Eddie. Are you hurt?'

'No,' he called back. 'I'm a bit stuck but I'm not hurt.' He lowered his voice so that only Jodie could hear him. 'I've never felt better, to be honest.'

He smiled down at Jodie and she smiled back.

She'd never felt better either. Her eyes were filling with tears again, but this time they were such happy tears they felt like liquid joy.

'I love you, Eddie...'

'I love you too, sweetheart.'

The sound of voices and the beams of torchlight were getting closer but...there was time for one more kiss before anyone broke this bubble, wasn't there?

Eddie answered her unspoken question instantly without saying a word.

Of course there was...

EPILOGUE

Three days later...

THE DAILY TEAM briefing of the Aberdeen Air Ambulance base had just finished and everybody had all the information they needed about weather conditions, levels of staffing and resources and potential disruptions to the shift. The last administrative team member was following Red Watch out of the meeting room and Dion was picking up his laptop computer when he noticed that Blue Watch wasn't moving.

'You guys on strike or something?'

'Jodie told us to hang around for a minute,' Gus said. 'I think she wants to say something.'

'I do.' Jodie nodded.

'Me too,' Eddie added.

Dion caught the look between the two paramedics and groaned. 'I hope it's not what I think it is,' he growled. 'I made myself very clear before you started work here, didn't I, Eddie?'

'You did,' Eddie acknowledged. 'Sorry, Dion…'

'What?' Alex was staring at Eddie. 'What have you got to be sorry about?'

Gus was staring at Eddie as well, but he wasn't looking bewildered like Alex.

'No way…' He was grinning. 'Are we talking shenanigans?'

'That's all it was supposed to be,' Eddie admitted. 'In which case we wouldn't have needed to confess anything. But…' He glanced at Jodie and clearly couldn't stop a smile spreading over his own face. 'Turns out it's a thing. The *real* thing.'

Jodie was smiling back at him. 'It is,' she confirmed. 'Definitely not shenanigans.'

'I don't believe it,' Gus said. 'And there I was thinking Jodie's job was more important to her than any relationship could ever be. What was it you said to me? "Been there, done that and never doing it again"?'

Jodie was trying—and failing—to stifle her grin. 'Things happen…' she murmured.

Dion was shaking his head. 'I don't believe it either. What's next? You're both going to go on holiday together and jump off the top of mountains? It was bad enough worrying whether Jodie would come home in one piece.'

'You don't have to worry about me,' Jodie told him.

'That's my job now,' Eddie added. 'I'm going to keep this amazing woman safe. Or die trying…'

'That's what I'm talking about,' Dion growled. 'Now I have to worry about losing my two best paramedics in one go.'

'Not if we're working on different watches,' Eddie pointed out. 'That's why we thought we'd better come clean and stop breaking the rules.'

Dion shaded his eyes with his hand. 'This is my fault, isn't it? I might have said it wasn't allowed but then I pushed you into each other's arms, didn't I? After that horrific job with the wedding accident. I told you to take Jodie out for a drink. To talk to her. To make her feel better…'

'He did.' Jodie's nod was solemn. 'He made me feel a lot better.'

'But that wasn't where it started,' Eddie assured him. 'It was actually where it was supposed to finish.'

'I had no idea,' Alex said. 'I just thought you guys liked working with each other.'

'We do,' they both said at the same time.

Jodie gave Dion a direct glance. 'I guess it kind of is your fault, though,' she said. 'It was you that talked us into doing that abseiling course last weekend and if it wasn't for that little whoopsie that Eddie had by the waterfall we might have just ignored how we really felt about each other.'

'A *whoopsie*…?' Dion could feel himself going a little pale. 'Do I want to know about what that entailed?'

'You really don't,' Eddie said firmly. 'And we've got more important things to talk about. We're due to start our shift in a few minutes and we can't keep working together, can we? Not when you made the rules so clear.'

'Well…it's not *exactly* a rule…' Dion's heart was sinking. The last thing he wanted to hear was that either Jodie or Eddie was planning to resign and work somewhere else.

'We're living together now,' Jodie put in. 'It's not as if we really need to spend every minute of every day together by working together as well.'

The look that passed between Eddie and Jodie suggested something very different, however. It was a look that brought a lump to Dion's throat, in fact. They loved each other, these two. At a level that most people could only dream about.

'You've moved in with Eddie?' Alex asked Jodie. 'That's going to be a bit of a squeeze in that wee basement apartment.'

'No. I've moved in with Jodie,' Eddie said. 'We came back from being together up in the mountains and decided that we were going to start the way we intend to spend the rest of our lives. Together...'

Both Alex and Gus were looking delighted.

'It's brilliant news,' Alex said. 'And I might know someone who can take over the apartment for you.'

'No need,' Eddie told him. 'My brother James is house-sitting for my sister Ella but they'll be back well before his locum at Queen's is due to finish. He's going to need a place of his own, especially if he decides to hang around a while longer after Mick gets back.'

'Sounds like things are falling into place nicely, then.' Gus nodded. 'It was meant to be.'

'It's all right for some,' Dion muttered. 'How am I supposed to deal with this? Swap one of you for someone on Red Watch?'

'You did say it wasn't exactly a rule,' Gus reminded him. 'And it's not as though any of us even noticed anything was going on. As far as we knew, they're the perfect team at work. The best... I don't want it to change.'

'Neither do I,' Alex said.

Neither did Dion, to be honest. Maybe he should just trust his instincts here.

'Fine,' he snapped. 'We'll leave things as they are, then. It's probably going to create more of an issue trying to separate you two than it would be letting you carry on working together.'

Man…just the glow from that glance that was passing between Eddie and Jodie now was like sunshine getting into the darkest corners ever.

They *were* the perfect team.

And he couldn't be happier for them.

'That's sorted, then,' he said gruffly. 'Let's get on with it, shall we?'

* * * * *

*Look out for the next story in the
Daredevil Doctors duet*

Rebel Doctor's Baby Surprise

*And if you enjoyed this story, check out
these other great reads from Alison Roberts*

Healed by a Mistletoe Kiss
The Italian, His Pup and Me
Fling with the Doc Next Door

All available now!